Birds and LANDS

Birds and LANDS

Kamrunnessa Kabir

BIRDS AND LANDS

This book is written to provide information and motivation to readers. Its purpose is not to render any type of psychological, legal, or professional advice of any kind. The content is the sole opinion and expression of the author, and not necessarily that of the publisher.

Printed in the United States of America.

ISBN 978-1-949746-67-9 (Paperback)
ISBN 978-1-949746-68-6 (Digital)

Lettra Press books may be ordered through booksellers or by contacting:

Lettra Press LLC
18229 E 52nd Ave.
Denver City, CO 80249
1 303 586 1431 | info@lettrapress.com
www.lettrapress.com

Monday evening Maria would be very excited to go to the park along with her only child Tito on the stroller in this nice summer evening. Finally, she has come to the end of her busy day. Busy with the children she takes care of along with her own son the two years old Tito. He's the one who keeps her busier. He's the one most demanding and notorious in contrary to those daycare children. They follow instructions to do things in the pattern of same daily routine. It doesn't seem they like the food always. Hungry or not they have to eat or leave the food all at the same time. They have to try to take a nap sleepy or not. While pretending to be sleeping by torturing themselves they tortured the person also who is watching them by managing her own son at the same time. Unlike them, Tito would be playing, sharing book reading or doing all other child activities with full pleasure, displeasure or by going with the heart with his own mother by giving her enough trouble. Like every other days Maria was busy cleaning their mess, running after them side-by-side doing her own household work. She keeps her spirit up while doing all at the same time. Watching children seems harder than anything to her. She cooked, she fed without feeding herself. She had to go to the grocery shopping also by pushing that two- story double bedded stroller in the Sun. The Summer Sunshine doesn't seem to be giving any comfort in such working hours. All five days of the week she works like a hyper steam machine onto fast wheels.

Now it's time to take a break in the nice summer weather in the park with her son. Mrs. Veronica will be there too from whom she borrows all of her exclusive outfits to look good to her husband Joseph. Joseph doesn't like particularly her this attitude. Borrowed costumes make a difference between him and his lovely wife as if a barrier between their real love. He loves Maria as she is. On the contrary Maria would say "I am all yours without all showing off". Joseph he's no less in arguing would pour out his love for her babe by saying I like to touch my beloved in her own Beauty and the best perfume ever ask of her own". Maria gets Naughty by twisting her eyebrows and squeezing her lips together to present a glimpse of her naughty smile. But again she also gets serious about the fact of getting along with the present life and the society by adopting some of it.

Time to go out. She got herself in the clothes and shoes she bought from a thrift store with her own money earned like that. She tries to provide her son clothes and things from better stores and never from a thrift store. Mom and son are free now in the nice light summer clothing. Maria's freedom is a break through the heard and bitter busy day. So the mother is enjoying the more than the Son. As always her mood also getting lost at the sight of her Old and torn stroller was also bought from a thrift store as well as her all accessories. Her watch seems to be ticking with her valuable time in the shameless boundary of her old cheap watch. The next moment thought "whatever"! And set out in the free nice summer breeze. While sitting on the bench in the park Maria looked around. The people around are from different cultures jogging, walking, running or having a little family picnic especially people like Maria. Community Gathering takes place mainly on weekends. Like many other children Tito also is playing around Maria while she's sitting alone on the bench. People are passing by. Some of them look at her and download a smile, some don't. Some of them gaze with suspicion or curiosity or even with some hatred. She's much more comfortable now. She knows various cultures and people now. She feels like another Stranger in the Land of strangers. Okay, people like Veronica seem friendly sometimes also very curious while nosy as well. This way she met Veronica one day. She's a nice lady friendly, open and caring. Tito goes along with her very nicely. She advises Maria how to dress him up in different weather accordingly, gives her a lot of information about lot of things she needs to know. The way she socializes makes Maria think how she knows how to survive with low income. Looks like these people come across everything as she is going through now. Maria looks at the present rich lady comes to the park to jog in expensive jogging suit and shoes while cares about covering Tito's bosom in cold wind and chill. She comes to the park only to jog doesn't look like very healthy. Thinks Maria sometimes Veronica as a rich lady must have been passed that time which Maria has been going through now. Maria's friend in the park looks much older than her but doesn't seem enjoying time much at her retirement. Time and place doesn't really vary things in reality

Maria came to the park just for an fresh air to breath and chill her temper while had been struggling with all the hyper active children along with her own free willed little child who happens to be as innocent as free of all worries. Maria as a loving mother as Nature made all mothers like that wishes him to be like that all his life ahead apparently denied by life itself which all have to live in its very lap loving it or just living it till the end. Children play, run, and jump not knowing falling into what while cautious adults die half worrying about all. "Whatever!" thinks Maria as she likes the tranquil time in the park. Most of the time she doesn't expect any companion until Joseph comes to pick her up after work. He always knows where she could be. At this summer time in the park and in winter time inside the mall at the walking distances.

She looks around sees people and the nurtured green of Nature. Despite the differences of appearance, language, color and the company they got with seem all happy and secure in a natural boundary above all. Whoever comes here most of them are different like her. They all must have taken the life here leaving the old one behind. Life seems better or looks better she doesn't know as she feels pain sometimes a pain for the soul. Maria thinks but not too much to go deep into the philosophy of life. May be there is none. Joseph and she are happy with love and care for each other. They do not really regret for whatever belongings they got for living. Whatever they have are precious for them for their love. Pain and gain always compensate each other no matter where we live. Tito is their love and hope for the new beginning if the life chain doesn't break again to start all over again. She got reckoned and shakes a little by the thought and blamed herself to think too much again.

Joseph is taking time to come this evening. Maria started longing for a company. Lot of people around but no one is in touch. Feels like 'water water everywhere not a drop to drink". Again it's too much of melancholy. She misses her family and friends back home. Unexpectedly when she was about to leave Veronica showed up. She took her sit beside her as usual and started talking about her busy life so and so much busy with essential gym, yoga, community club, and of course doctors. She started talking how busy she was. How busy she is in her luxury time might be with luxury items not with luxury to live and feel. Sometimes Maria thinks why she comes to the park to relax which is a public place is apparently for and with people like Maria. Definitely for fresh air might be also for a company but why.

Handing out some chocolates to Tito Veronica asked "is your husband coming now to pick you up?" "Yes in 10 minutes" Maria's answer. "Good! I like that. But you can also try to go to some nearby community centres sometimes. They have daycare centers too for children. You can talk to people and also do some volunteer jobs while putting your son there. I mean, of course it's your life Veronica murmured. Maria answers everything she says and never asks anything. The local lady asking "what did you cook for dinner tonight?" "Just some chicken to go with bread". "You can cook daal sometimes I know your people cook a lot of that it's delicious and healthy". Some people here like to give her solutions to alternatives of food cheaper than the other one. They have a lot of suggestions about the way of living by saving money. If Maria was in her country presently she would have been taking this as an insult or discrimination but here everybody seems very practical. They'll even grow by counting pennies luxury and vanities have their own time. She Relies on Veronica's guidelines. Good to have someone to talk and share information in a land not known before in detail. Maria's foreign friend is very curious about her life style. She wants to know almost about everything about her family. She also appreciates Maria's food the food they cook in the community. But she never accepts an invitation from her. On the other hand, Maria never dare to ask about her personal and family life. She even doesn't ask how many family members she has. Maria feels like she can only ask her about her health condition. These two different friends from two different worlds are like two parallel rail lines merging side by side without touching each other never and forever. Might be the hearts of the two different passengers would be the same. Maria appreciates Veronica's softness the way she loves and cares about her son.

Maria got up as soon as she saw Joseph coming towards her. And Veronica her company cheers 'there you go! He is here! You have a lovely family what else is desirable other than love? Look! How much he cares about you!" Maria and Joseph both got shy and Joseph smiled a bit. After Josephs "hi" Veronica also joked by saying 'I was with your beautiful wife'. "Never leave a beautiful wife alone you never know". "I only have one". All laughed at Josephs comment. Veronica had a little chat with Joseph about some business and job opportunities. She is always curious about his career. She likes to show them some paths to opportunities. Looks like she would have been included Joseph in her own company if still she was running it. She talks about how to get the counter for jobs, what aspects make a business, how to run a business, how to manage a property and about all the systems there. And for Joseph as an immigrant how to survive in the first place. He's eager to learn and Veronica likes to continue talking ignoring the fact that Maria is waiting to leave with Joseph or might have been even forgotten the fact that she was there.

At some point Joseph stops talking to listen only by looking at his family to catch her attention. Both husband and wife never says "we have to go" or" have got to go" with an apology. Instead always Veronica says "sorry" for keeping them long when she realizes the couple got tired and needs to leave for home. Sometimes she walks with them to the parking lot. Maria always wonders at her nice, handsome apparently a very expensive car Joseph always wishes to have one like that kind. And he always jokes "here is the Prince Charming Chariot! Lets Princess! Let's go to our sweet home." Joseph likes her wonder and hidden desires taken as an inspiration to do better for better. Off to the driving home happily and cheerfully

Maria got the surprise to hear that her loving partner for the night to relax and sleep says "I have to leave now for a job interview I have no time left to go inside."

"How about dinner?" Maria asked by concealing the complaint she has against a certain breakdown of a regular routine.

"I'll have something to eat outside you eat with Tito and take care. Sorry I did not get a chance to talk about it. Take it easy my Dear! No hard feelings". Saying this he left quickly without looking back to his family knowing and feeling the heart of his wife only by saying those words to his love. Mario thought a bit by holding her sons hand and approached inside to the elevator for home accepting the fact of change at the change of time and place. By feeding and sending Tito to bed Maria was still awake to see Joseph home as worried about his arrival at home sweet home after all his hard work for them.

Joseph did not come that late but looked tired and cheerful at the same time in his expression when he said "You know I needed an extra part time job as I used to talk about. My colleague informed about an opportunity and I took the chance in a very short time isn't good Maria? Don't worry nothing is permanent yet we will have better opportunities and better life.' 'He hugged and kissed her with love and the hope in his eyes to give hope to his love his Maria. Maria didn't say anything just gazed at the special new movie she borrowed for tonight to watch together by casting a gaze against Joseph's tired Body and Soul as well as hers then quickly went to bed they have work tomorrow.

Still Maria is staying up trying to sleep beside her sleeping husband in bed. She didn't expect a Bed of Roses but at least a bed to have a sound sleep after working hard all day long with lots of worries. Most of the nights she could not sleep. She pines for Joseph's company after work and tonight she is a bit more upset at his plan to do over time. It's not good for his health as well as for their conjugal life. It's true he is trying for good for better future she herself also doesn't pine or die for expensive things or luxury. She prefers living in limits with love and care. She cares about living a healthy life. As an educated woman she understands reality but still she values her home with values and love. She wishes things and places that are valuable but she values real value only and not vanity at all as she doesn't regret ending up in MacDonald after being viewed the Reinforest.

She can see Bindi front door apartment neighbor, she can see Cynthia the corner unit neighbor who shares the children by dividing the time of day and night between both her husband and herself as a dutiful-time sharing proper wife properly for the requirement of time. The mother takes care of the baby when the father is at work and the father does the same when the mother is at work. In this routine of life for the sake of money to fuel the life the child gets care, the parents commit duties but does the time share give them enough time to share a life together as family? She sees single parents also around her. She feels better as she sees single parents all by themselves. At least she lives together with her family. In the phase of her 25 years' life time she has gotten enough experiences, experience of the fear of wars, insecurities, hardship and struggle to get on her own heels. But still the life breathes. Maria and Joseph got hope as well as energy from their love, friendship, family and friends. Life is not that much cruel to ban all of its refreshments. It still peeps with the beam of some enjoyment through its shattered structure.

Maria and Joseph enjoy all the Wonders here, all attractions museums, fun parks, site seeing etc. They enjoy food outside different than theirs. Beyond all the good and bad of their present life in the foreign land with new reality they thrive, get ambitious but veronica's life style and her riches make Maria more curious rather than to be ambitious. The rich lady's appearance with all her stories is more of a relief in her laborious days less of a dream to dip in or to aspire by forgetting reality. She's not as dumb as to be fooled by fake life and its luxury. Despite of all Veronica's stories of luxury lifestyle Maria gets curious of her real life.

Saturday morning. Maria took all the dirty clothes to the laundry down in the lobby by holding a hand of Tito and another by pushing the cart. Joseph is out at work. He works some extra hours on weekends as the store got busier than before. He was also late last night for Maria's birthday as he might be forgotten her birthday. She cooked special food and dressed up nice doesn't matter no dinner out no birthday gift as well. It's her birthday. When he came home tired and exhausted failed to notice any differences in his wife's appearances or in the spirit she got on the special day. Maria didn't mention about her birthday as she knows he's working hard to be tired, exhausted and cranky sometimes. She served dinner and started eating together. By noticing Joseph's good mood while got glad about the delicious food tonight to thank Maria with love and affection Maria asked with a little cheer "did you forget something tonight?" But Joseph startled with a worry and asked "what? Doctor's appointment? Why didn't you tell me before? I could manage to take some time off!" to this kind of reaction in that state of mind what could Maria say but Just to keep quiet. This is for the first time that Joseph forgot her birthday. She thought "oh well, busy life!" and then concentrated on consuming the food tonight. But still love prevails. All in a sudden her husband seemed looked up for a clue for something missing something dear and loving to cheer to say "wait a minute, did I miss something? What date is this? Oh! God it's your birthday Maria! Sorry my dear! My love come to me" to hug and kiss her the very next moment. He hugged and loved his wife as if also got rid of a smoky exhaustion of the day on so-called busy life for a relief. However, the next day that Sunday has been fixed for luxury dinner and shopping apparently to buy a gift for the birthday girl.

Luckily she finished doing laundry before the laundry room gets crowded so much. As usual this morning also Maria did not miss meeting Lianna who happens to borrow money from her not to return ever again in spite of all her promises with a smoking smoke 'swear to God I will return the Looney as soon as possible". Looking again into Maria's eyes would say 'I promise I'll give you all back...I'll give all together I promise". Maria doesn't mind that young lady anymore. She knows she makes promises not to keep may be in her conscience not to break.

By the time she finished doing all the laundry the corridor became crowded. The neighborhood seems to be awakened and alive again with a pause paw of the night gone. Maria got upset at the thought of being awaited for a long time for the elevator. Tito is crying uncomfortable since the morning with a pause of and on to release his mother a bit from an annoying situation. It's 11.00

am. Already. The laundry room will be crowded too thought Maria. These kinds of situations and environment remind her of the house back home. She has a past which she doesn't really claim to be nice and beautiful. If it was so they wouldn't be here. Her father died in a sudden Blast in the neighborhood and her brother was captured as a prisoner from a rally never to come back again. Tito cried loud to break her thoughts while wandering into the memory of the past happy or not but certainly of her own and close to the heart and soul. Shouting and sweating of a neighbor from an apartment across the corridor also started a little her soft bosom. Who is shouting God knows for what reason. People break peace like that not even living in a war. "Life is all about Misery" she thinks "almost most of the part" However, people are surviving in the middle of all these and they're also in her country in Wars forever. She thinks fish like people manage themselves to jump up the fire into the frying pan might be again to jump out to reach a better place to survive. She wonders after facing so much trauma and getting so much pain how can people like her and Joseph is to live with hope and desire still. Sometimes the heart dies quietly without letting the body know while the soul reckons. Sometimes the body keeps going with its chemistry only.

Half of the summer has been passed with a fear of its decay. Whatever, time doesn't sit so do the life? People move up with plans and guts, thrive and work for better for a future. They work real hard and thrive to survive in a foreign land. Tito is grown up a little more as a School boy. It is time for Maria to do something better. She's planning to do some study to upgrade for a better job. Dear friendships and relationships grew bigger to share, care and to enjoy. Joseph and Maria's friends and relatives are also moving on with the trends here. They communicate; they share information and time and care for each other. They go out together, they sit together, and they celebrate and party together. They enjoy, they live by emptying the heart of pain to each other. But they also compete very subtle to improve themselves over one another. All of these sharing and caring is nothing but passion to bring hope and dream.

It's August already. Summer will be over soon. In the past two months Maria came to the park a few times but could not see Veronica. She thinks of her only when she comes to the park because she misses her then as a company. Last time when she met Veronica she was very busy hurrying to leave saying that her boyfriend was waiting in the car. Maria got surprised by looking at the elderly looking lady having a boyfriend while married all along. Usually boyfriend thing goes with the young girlfriend. Maria got confused "doesn't she also have a husband?" oh, well! Luckily she met Veronica today.

As soon as she met she picked up Tito as well as always. Thought Maria again "doesn't she have a child?" She never asked Veronica about her personal life, never ever questioned about her family, or her business whatever information she got about her were delivered by Veronica herself in the conversation with Maria. All she talks about her mom, her sisters, about party, official meetings, about going to the doctor's or going on a vacation etc. Most of the times she leaves by saying "I'll go see my sister to go shopping together" and arriving by saying "I have dropped my mom after visiting her doctor on the way here-----. She started the conversation today by saying 'you look different today. You are beautiful, does Joseph say that to you? He loves you!" Maria got shy with eyes down with a smile and Veronica looked at her significantly to ask her about her stunning bracelet 'is it from your place? "yes, an anniversary gift" Maria's answer. The foreign lady said then it again with an inspirational mind cheerfully 'he loves you! And then also got a little bit absent-minded looking a far away.

Veronica always is curious about Maria's conjugal life so does Maria about Veronica's. The difference is Maria never asked anything about Veronica's. Each time she learns more about her only from whatever information she delivers for her. Maria tends to learn more about Veronica and her lifestyle. Is it the Curiosity about a different person? or the curiosity about the land and its culture with an inner excitement to know the unknown or might be a little fear inside to be get lost or lose her own in a land got driven by fate or ambition. On the other hand, Veronica seems more interested in Maria's personal life rather than her culture. Maria got very surprised today when the next moment Veronica asked 'does your husband sleep with other women?' a very surprising indeed! Maria got very annoyed but answered like before said "no". And then the rich local lady asked 'do your people do that?" "Not generally. There are bad apples everywhere". Maria didn't know how she became so wise today by thinking that the issue and the answer might be Veronica's own weakness.

Winter evenings are boring and sometimes unbearable being stuck high on a high-rise apartment building with Tito's hyper behavior, jumping on furniture, running around, screaming loud demanding for things, turning on and off the TV again and again all kinds of hyper child activities keep her busy and restless. After he Goes back to sleep she would start cleaning the mess, and prepare dinner for her and Joseph. If Joseph comes late he would eat alone and find a room to sleep beside the sleeping wife. Sharing some time with love and Companionship happens only when Joseph comes home early. Maria likes to think of herself as a bird living in a nest up on a big tree with her mate. But no, this home is not a nest in open air to fly from anywhere to any place, any time. This lodging is their Freehold captivity. They live, they thrive for their own good by their own energy.

A little less chill today. Maria is setting out with all the children to the park Love to play in the snow making snowballs, snowman Etc. For Maria is good to see the 'Snow White Mother Nature' when it is a less cold to tolerate. She doesn't Envy the Free birds anymore as they also can't fly much in the snowy weather. Well, human life had been and has been involved in a lot of migration from here to there, from Coast to Coast no matter what to be and what the causes are.

Kids are busy playing while Maria's mind set on the evening after they leave. She has to prepare the food items marinated and chopped to prepare tomorrow. Another Saturday in winter tomorrow. Maria and Joseph invited some friends. Winter time not much going out. They see each other by inviting one another randomly on weekends. Most of the ladies of her communities have taken courses to study for a job. Tito is still little Maria has to stay home with him. She will have to go for a long time study for a career. Time and money both are holding her back.

Watching soap opera on TV from the kitchen makes her very curious about the characters and the ups and downs in their lives. They look all pretty and handsome in rich living and background but they are never happy because of the inconsistency in relationships, Love and Marriage as well as in business. If these kinds of Dramas are the portrayal of real rich people are they really living constantly in inconsistency looking beautiful and okay? That stylish look and behavior of the series' characters with luxury might be more or less exists in reality which reminds her about Veronica. She didn't see her long time. If she had her phone number would she call Veronica sometimes? May be not because the sky and the ground Seem meeting together far away in the horizon but they are always away from each other far and Far up and down.

Someone knocking at the door Maria hurried and walks towards the door wondering who might be there at this time and to her surprise it was none but Veronica herself standing in front of her at the open door of whom she just thought about. What a coincidence! She got rid of all her shyness and the distance she always keeps between herself and her foreign friend and screamed with joy at once 'it's you! What a co-incidence! I just thought about you. How did you know my place? You just dropped me here only once which was a long time too good memory!" by saying so many words at a time in a single breath with so much excitement and happiness Maria got a little shy and got polite again said 'Please come in. good to see you. How is everything?"

"No, no I am fine. I just came to invite you to my place for Christmas. This year I have invited a lot of other people including my company employees. You will see my sister and my mother also.

I hope you don't mind". Veronica also replied all in one breathe in hurry. She doesn't have any intention to come inside. "Sure! I will try my best. Thank you for inviting me to your special event up to go."

"It will be very special if all of you join together. Christmas is no longer a Christmas with family and friends. People use the holidays nowadays for vacations. I don't blame people and I don't blame us time changing. Anyway, trying to keep up the tradition. Last few years I celebrated the big day only with my mother and sister." This is the first time Veronica disclosed herself a bit more to Maria. A Rich lady possessing a big mansion and a big company feeling lonely means a lot to Maria. With all the establishments and the luxury, the rich lady missing the charms of her own culture and Society made Maria feels a bit better somehow. By remaining calm and quiet Maria said again 'I would love to see your party, your arrangements and all. Thank you again for including me."

"You are coming for sure right? Veronica asked again." yes, of course but I have to check with Joseph."

"O, yea, come with the family. Call me to make sure." By saying these last words or making sure of the invitation to the whole family Veronica walked out by giving her phone number on a little piece of paper. She came all in a sudden also left in hurry by delivering a message in shorter time with least possible courtesies without showing any more interest in Maria or Tito's well being or in their little home to see or in a bit more chat. Maria still was holding the door looking at Veronica's walk away. A little while ago she got overwhelmed by her warm welcome to her house and now the very next moment she got confused about the invitation by a foreign friend to an unknown event with basically all new people.

7 days to go for the party in Veronica's house. Maria is excited. They are going as a family since Joseph won't have to go to work on that day. She is going to wear a proper party dress as known as to be for a party in the place. She feels a bit guilty for going to be like them in their kind of dress and then change to think that looking alike doesn't seem to be being alike. She spent a lot of time in shopping looking for a perfect Christmas gift for a rich lady within her capacity.

Finally, the day arrived. All of them got dressed in black Joseph in black suit as well as Tito and Maria in black with a lot of nice jewelleries going with her black party dress. She looked beautiful and stunning as a lady as always as to look attractive. They all set out at 5 p.m. Feeling great with a little fear to come back with the same greatness from a party or an event not known yet especially with all strangers.

Veronica's grand house looks like a palace with all the decorations and lighting around. The front yard looks gorgeous with the lighted trees shining and smiling. Big Look and a big smiling welcome with a shine with lights to the guests tending them to enter the very door of the house at the very end through the path way made them feel a little strange and exciting at the same time. For a moment when she felt like they are insignificant and improper in such a place. When she took a look at Joseph at the same he looked at her with the same impression and the thoughts. After passing the yard proceeding towards the grand house with a lot of confusions they got received with a warm welcome by a charming lady who opened the grand door first with a very charming smile and welcoming words of all times. It was very inviting and welcoming with heart well enough to make these new guests very comfortable.

The hallway seemed very crowded at first. Later all the guests took their sits here and there in the rooms, in the dining space, in the living room or in the family room. Maria also with other ladies to be seated in the family room with all of them and Joseph somewhere upstairs, Tito started playing around with other children. Some people were climbing up and down stairs.

Veronica came out of the kitchen with a smile open armed to hug all the guests. She picked up Tito also as usual. Veronica's courtesy to welcome the new guests along with her love and affection made the new guests easy and comfortable. Maria started to look around and her eyes up and down with still some shyness and hesitation. She's lifting her eyes to see people and down when they see secret criticism in the eyes of some people. Maria thought these people must be the host's close relations and Friends. They changed to look at her appearance attitude and different complexion.

Maria and Joseph felt better when they met some other aliens like them. Veronica came in chef gown from the kitchen to guide Joseph to the living room where most of the men were sitting. Maria looked around the house to view the big open kitchen with gorgeous marble counter tops, expensive appliances and gorgeous wooden shelves. As standing between the family room and the kitchen she looked inside the big living room through the door near the kitchen and the hallway. She also took a look at the nice aristocratic marble floor all over and at the big spiral stairs going up must be to some more rooms. She wished for a moment to see more of the upstairs but thought of sitting with other ladies in the family room of what needs to be performed at that moment as a guest in the party. Veronica asked for an excuse to enter the kitchen again saying there are still some things left to be done by her. Maria was standing in the same spot for the time by holding the hands of her son as was still not asked to be sited. The very moment she took her seat though in a nice and soft sofa with all the ladies looked alike.

While sitting in the family room with the ladies of different complexions apparently from different backgrounds like her. All of the ladies introduced themselves to one another by telling their names only. Some started talking in a pair, some of them in a group. And Maria got a chance to talk to a lady look skinny and beautiful with the brown complexion in a nice tight dress down up to the knee. She sat beside Maria and asked her by introducing herself as Papri 'Maria right?" "Yes" Marias humble answer.

The next question of the lady towards Maria is 'how long you have been living here?"

"Just three years".

"Do you like it here?"

As Maria was going to answer Papri's question Veronica came to intervene by telling Maria that she's going to take Tito to the basement with all other children. They will see Santa there and have lots of fun with toys later to open Santa's gifts for Christmas. After Veronica and Tito are gone Papri asked Maria 'what do you do in Christmas? Did you celebrate Christmas with friends and family last years here?"

"We don't celebrate Christmas."

"Oh sorry! Papri's answer with an apology again to ask the very next question "are you working now or not yet. I guess going to school? You might have been educated from your own country."

"Yes we go to school in our country and I am a graduate".

"Of course! Here newcomers to go to school for a training for career. Have you already taken a course?"

"For now I'm just a home daycare provider this way I can see my own child too"

"Of course, children are priority. But you know children will always occupy you. If I were you I would have gone for Career build-up by putting the child in a daycare center." by saying these the Charming lady left to get a drink.

"She must be an official" thought Maria while feeling herself down at the same.

"Are you Maria? An elderly white lady definitely not from the place where they all are residing.

"Yes. And you are----------" answered Maria with some hesitations.

"Eugenia, living here for 20 years. And you------ oh yes, I met your people don't your ladies put on scarf?" looking into Maria's eyes said Eugenia "okay I'm just asking. You are beautiful and looking gorgeous this way". The elderly lady continued talking and said again to ask Maria.

"You knew English before. You did. So you can do things here too!" looks like she's curious and worried at the same time. Thought Maria again 'why these ladies are so concerned about her career. Isn't it what to do her own business?" The old lady seemed very affectionate and caring at the same time look like showing pity on her by offering a drink to Maria getting it from the other side of the room by leaving her own seat beside Maria. Maria got uneasy again with the concern of her difference in the existing differences of all these ladies in the foreign land. Eugenia continued answering Maria with her talk or Maria's still unspoken answers to her said 'you don't drink alcohol right? Sorry I go get a soft drink for you".

All the ladies she met in the family room are from different cultures like Maria. Like all the ladies her complexion is also fair except Papri. She must be a south Asian. It's not fair to pointing out each other's origin in detail to Maria it makes a difference. Many others maintained the courtesy very tactfully just like her. They all know Veronica for a long time some of them are working for her in her company. They all are pretty and adjacent to the present culture and proudly getting along with Veronica and her close relatives and Friends. They could tell that Maria is new in the country some of them are boasting by saying that they know Veronica for a long time some of them playing a leadership role by helping the host in various matters, some of them showing pity on her by coming to know her as a new immigrant along with her ethnicity. Detained to tell her the ways to shop, how to cook, to dress up according to the weather condition or how to take care of her son. Apparently Maria is the most beautiful lady in the event tonight. Some of them look like wandering at her beauty when they look at her. Some of them are not happy to see her and look at her with the pale face what is poised both eyebrows together as if her presence is very disturbing and annoying. Some ladies especially elders are being too nice to her by helping her at every turn like where to sit, which appetizer to take and where is the washroom etc.

They all are loud, cheerful, boasting at some points, very active to take a leadership role to help each other especially a poor lady like Maria apparently nice and shy and quiet at the same time. Maria knows by now how to dress up like them that dressing up like them did not make her behaving like them. Even without knowing her they can tell that she is a newcomer, naive with a different culture. In the meantime, Veronica came downstairs in her party looking very gorgeous in an outfit down up to the knee. Veronica's nice black dress is different than the others for its sophistication of the fabric and the embroidery and of course the expense for it which everyone can tell. The glow less nice shine of the diamonds on her body was catching everyone's eyes other than her own. Ladies are always great to boast and to die and fall on beauty and the boast.

Veronica appeared with a beauty to boast with the hair done high up from the parlor looked like a Queen to make them complement almost all in the same feminine expressions with these kinds of words 'oh my God! Look at you! You look gorgeous! All fabulous! By hugging her to say 'Merry Christmas! They also discussed about her expensive outfit and the Diamonds by judging the price, beauty and from which sophisticated store was it bought.

Maria was still silent and watchful in the crowd. For the first time she noticed Veronica's sharp uplifted nose a little above the blood red lips with red lipstick and her tired and pale eyes in dark eye makeup underneath her bare blonde forehead. The less talkative Maria just said 'you look very beautiful" while is the gorgeous host passing by. She started to wonder at Veronica's active management of the whole party things, the big Gathering, nice and clean big house, working at the kitchen and maintaining all the guests with proper manners.

By leaving the rest of the charges of the kitchen on the shelf or on the lady helpers Veronica came back to Maria and introduced her to her mom and sister. Despite her age the mother looked Beautiful and bright dressed up almost in the same way as the daughter. The old lady smiled nicely to say" hi Maria! My daughter talks about you a lot. You are a nice lady. My daughter is very kind and social she makes friends with all kinds of people. She helped a lot of people to get a job. You see all of these ladies most of them are working in her company. She's got her dad's Talent. He was the founder of the company and my Veronica carried on very nicely. With a deep sigh to pause a bit the mother added "well, now she got her retirement doesn't like to work so hard anymore. My son-in-law he's in charge now my daughter is still looks after from home sometimes attending some important meetings. You know what, I'm very proud of my daughters they both are like two parts of my heart. I don't have a son. Well I don't regret. they are trouble you know! Boys look only after outside world. My girls are always close to me as they Care and Share a lot. Here, meet my other daughter Mary". The proud old mother introduced Mary her younger daughter to Maria and Maria said 'hi' to her with a smile. Mary looked back to overlook as an opposite nature of the mother who seemed to be a lot more open and friendly.

Veronica came back to say "mom, its 8 o'clock I think we should serve the dinner but Victoria did not show up yet. Should I wait a bit more for her?"

Mrs. Scott got a bit annoyed by making her face one of a kind to show a tiny bit of hatred not really in very true sense 'I hate these High Society people they don't really care about the hosts waiting for them. I don't know whether they are real busy or like to be careless. Don't value the Christmas dinner to be taken together. They are losing the values and the glory of the holiday. Good Lord! What else would I see in my last days of life". Three ladies Veronica, her mom and Maria fell into the conversation to decide whether to call the very important or the chief guest again to check whether she is on the way or just to wait maximum half an hour more.

Ladies are still talking seem to be not hungry at all just like Maria herself. Sitting alone in a corner by watching the chirping lady crowd seems like a bit of fun in relaxation. She doesn't know how much time has been past viewing all the lady guests their dresses, jewelleries, watches, high heels, makeup and hair along with the subject matters they talked about. Their English accents, Their Manners, the way they talk and behave is very noticeable to Maria as if she's trying to learn or just to observe. Suddenly they all got up going somewhere else in the house. Before knowing anything she followed them too heading upstairs to see the rest of the house.

The entered veronica's bedroom first. A pretty spacious room with luxury windows beside the luxury bed, dresser mirror, chest and two luxurious sofas to sit. Maria went close to the picture of Veronica with her husband a big photo in a big frame on the wall with names written on the foot Mr. And Mrs. Peter Brown. Maria recognized her husband this is the man who was walking silent around downstairs didn't seem to be much talkative. A lot of times she caught his sight seemed looking at her especially. Maria wondered about the mystery of Veronica's having a boyfriend while together with her husband smiling in the photo. Maria saw her boyfriend only once seems less handsome than the husband. They entered the washroom which is also a showpiece Jacuzzi, luxurious glass shower place, nice marble counter-top under the shiny and good looking glass with especial luxury bulbs on top. While she took a look with a lot of interest at the Jacuzzi Mary looked at her very critically and said "you know this is called Jacuzzi. Did you hear about this before?" Maria understood her position in such a grand place therefore she remained silent.

They visited four more bedrooms well decorated but not as luxurious as Verona's. Marry left when they were in the room where there was a teenage boy's photo on the wall. Standing in front of the picture a lady remarks 'did you see a teenage girl's picture also in the other room? I'm wondering if they are Verona's children. Another lady said 'if they are her children where are they I did not see them today." the other lady of these ladies kind said 'people, I never saw them before or heard about anything about her children from veronica's mouth. I knew her for 3 years good Lord!"

There were two other ladies as of Veronica's people spoke out very quickly to defend the host 'they might be with her first husband". Still the former three ladies started whispering among themselves like this "she lives alone without her children?"

"Good Lord!'

Hearing them like this the defendant said again "they must be sharing both parents".

All the ladies sighed with a mean pale face to say 'AH!' Together. Leaving them behind whispering and criticizing the host behind her, Maria walked ahead to see The Corner Room. The room looks like a little family Library seems doesn't get much sunlight during daytime as the windows we're covered half by the book shelves. Maria hesitated a bit and then started to look at the room walking from the left to the right from the entrance. The wall above the shelves were well decorated with some nice artwork of paintings. She randomly looked at the Books to see what kinds of collections were there.

There are varieties economics, finance, business, literature, history, politics, biographies, lot of novels and story books and much more. Someone must be bookish or knowledge thirsty here but who? Veronica or her husband?

"Can I help you?" someone asked from behind while she became a little thoughtful. Maria looked around to face the person who is nobody but the short Quiet Man known as Veronica's husband. As she faced the left side of the room she noticed the single bed and the table chair as well fitted in the study room. But she doesn't know whether the short man was here all the time or just arrived. Mr. Brown smiled very thin from a corner of his closed lips Maria doesn't know what language it says. 'What is this beautiful young lady doing in the most boring room?' he asked.

"Nothing, just looking around".

"Did you find anything interesting here? A cunning way to say more "there is no showcase full of beautiful things or eye catching posters. Books do not look nice". Maria got very embarrassed at his way of talking and answered in a very low voice "I was just looking at the books kept here".

Mr. Peter examining an object game said, 'what did you see? Name some of them."

Maria doesn't know whether she is uttering or murmuring some weak words or letters to defend herself started it pronouncing 'Homer, Somerset Maugham, Shakespeare, Wordsworth, George Bernard Shaw, Dale Carnegie---------- "so do have some education where are you from?"

Maria couldn't tell whether Mr. Brown was insulting her or encouraging her. As about to say something Mr. Brown asked her again 'did you read Homer?"

"No" answered Maria.

"You just know. Did you read Shakespeare? You must have read some.'

"I know the story of Shylock and Romeo Juliet".

"Romeo Juliet ha! How! Do you like The Love Story?" at this point veronica's husband came closer when Maria realized that she was talking to a drunk man all while ago. Before anything anymore, she got dragged towards Mr. Brown as he already got hold of her by holding her left hand to browse her neck area with the other hand whispering 'did you read the story "the diamond necklace"? What is your diamond necklace?" before he's hand goes more down Maria shook herself off to run away from the unexpected ghost at the wrong time in a wrong place.

All the ladies we're already gone downstairs without seeing The Corner Room. Running down hot flushed Maria noticed that dinner was already served. Confused Maria doesn't know where to go or sit. She seems to be unnoticed by the busy people there. No one asked where she was. She took her seat back in the family room. In such a big house with so much Arrangements no one is aware of what has just happened. Maria doesn't know the word 'harassment' yet all she felt is insult and fear. Her feelings gave her a shake with the fear of what would have happened if she could not get out of there. Nobody around the panting Maria sitting alone in that room didn't really know for how long. Might be for a short time. Veronica's showed up to be surprised to see her there all alone said, 'there you are! Didn't you go for dinner? Go eat. Tito is fine I put him in a chair. He should be fine go check on him'.

The host guided her to the big dining room. Guests were taking food from the table and sitting somewhere in the room. Those ladies who she met before earlier in the family room walked back to the room again to be sited to eat. At the very end of the big table it was Veronica's mom sitting to watch all at the same time to watch all to have her own dinner as well. Maria happens to be pleased by seeing her son sitting in the nearest chair of the old lady. As soon as Maria gladly walked towards her son he drops some pieces of chicken on the carpet along with some more mess. The lady most probably kin to The Host cast an angry look at her and commanded softly, 'pick it up'. Maria got very embarrassed and guilty in front of all the people looking at her son and herself. "Might be not', thought Maria all are busy having dinner". While she got very busy to find a way very quickly to clean the mess a lady from the kitchen came forward with lot of respect to clean instead of Maria also said, 'sorry, I thought I could feed your child while I did not see you. Go take him somewhere to feed. Don't worry about the mess. Someone will clean the rest."

Some of the guests lifted their eyes up for a moment to see the mess as well as the boy who caused it and his mother hard to tell with hatred or not but definitely not very happy or got very disturbed by the mess in the middle of the dinner. The whole situation to Maria is nothing but enormous embarrassment while her son was still constantly talking and singing to make the mess more annoying to the people there and more embarrassing two Maria. She had to snatch out Tito from his seat to get out of there to be seated somewhere else. Nobody cares except Mrs. Scott said kindly to Maria, 'go to the kitchen table to feed him and also yourself". Some ladies we're already there feeding the children along with some housekeepers helping some other children to feed on behalf of their mother.

Maria took a look at the open space near where Joseph was eating and chatting with other guests. Here in the kitchen nobody cared who came late or what happened before. Maria also took a seat to be fed and feed. For her observation was more than enjoying the event. All of the human behaviors, manners, attitudes are normal as universal by the time and place. People always behave the same always and almost everywhere. Only the incidence in the library room kept her mind occupied with hatred, shame and fear. This couldn't be expected from an unknown party like this. The most gorgeous woman Veronica is around. Maria was watching this beautiful lady also with all thc luxury and Riches looking empty and tired from her look instead of all the makeup, all the beauty with nice jewelry in a nice dress on such a grand party. The single bed in the little room upstairs and the frustrated behavior of a husband shows how happy she is in her personal life. The beautiful and the Proud Lady of the time look like a Walking Dead beauty without a soul.

The dinner was over ladies we're back again to chat and relax with the taste of desert. By finishing feeding Tito Maria also took some desert. No one knew that she did not have main course except the old lady. She even asked her whether she could bring a plate for her. Maria excused and got herself busy again in answering various questions asked by the ladies. They tend to be curious about each other than caring about each other. They notice how everybody dressed up among themselves, their accents, their English, their way of talking and manners, their family background, and of course they're very personal lives and status. The mom sighed sitting beside Maria to say 'what are they! No prayer no dinner together! No Christmas in a true sense! Go take your son to the Santa. He will enjoy having a present like all other children. Good Lord! No blessing! No wishing only Gathering not knowing for what!" For the first time Maria noticed that the jingle bell song is playing in a nice and soft tune behind all the crowd in the party.

Maria looked very happy seeing all the children having fun in the basement. Her Tito joined them too very playful. She stood there for quite some time to see her Tito having fun with the children where there is the Santa an angel from the Holy Land of gifts, a playmate of wishes to deliver to the innocent children. A foreign lady like her being a mother what can she expected more than his betterment in the foreign land. She's very happy for now to see her son enjoying the same like all other children.

She came back upstairs where there the ladies where is still chatting with more volume and cheer. Including her they are all from different heritage, and countries happen to be different in colors and behavior may be the different looks also to make one big tree holding different fruits of colors and beauty. Maria is new but all others here looking the same with same ways of talking, sitting with same language and gesture. They all speak the same language with different accent. They started talking about work, school, daycare, shopping, home management as well as the busy life. At this point they all seem very realistic in real life by sharing the life experiences together.

The very next moment the male guests in the other room became very loud in talking about politics, social systems, present economy and all the problems in the systems. On the other hand, here in the ladies' room they started to gossip about husband, children with a deep sigh or a happy smile. Gossiping of shopping made them very interested and gossiping Vacations Made Them very excited. Finally, they came back to Beauty care with all love and care. Maria is still coming quiet not much to say or comment. This time also Papri looked at her specifically asked by sitting beside her 'your hair is long and silky mine was too. But here I chopped It Off. Hard to maintain."

Another lady also added 'what do you use for your hair? Your skin is nice too. How do you take care of it?" without waiting for the answers to those questions she left for her former sit by saying "you are beautiful. aren't you?" but another lady insisted to know the care of her skin and hair as having herself a very rough skin and hair without any moisture or shine said, 'which shampoo you use and how many times a week?' "Any shampoo doesn't actually look at the brands. I have just stopped using soaps". And the lady got very surprised almost a scream to raise the next question the very next moment 'how about your skin? Have you seen a beautician already? I know someone can help you." when the answers we're no to any of those questions the lady lost interest in talking to the new comer who knows from what part of the world!" she just walked away by saying these words to Maria with the nicest smile" Nature fade away and care helps to keep the beauty as long as possible'.

From the Smile of the lady Maria didn't know how to take those words as an advice or a malice. But again the very next moment the caring or the Curious blonde lady came back to ask 'I noticed some tiny blue spots on your face, neck and shoulder and what are they?" all the ladies looked back to take a careful look at Marias face with the most wonder and curiosity of all. "From a dynamite to blast not very far from me" Maria's this short answer is well enough to make them all scream again this time all together as a chorus "blast! You mean Bomb Blast? Where? When?" the storyteller's story as follows as when Maria was playing in front of her apartment building at her very young age when she got those blue spots from the Smoky Spark of a blast happened to be very often around the neighborhood.

The told story seemed very shocking to the ladies and they all came back to her with sympathy and with curiosity at the same time to learn and know more about her stories from the past. Well there was nothing more to know about those places from where Maria came from. They just sighed wondered and criticized. The blond came close to the victim this time to introduce herself which she did not do a while ago said, 'I'm Kathy by the way. How long you have been living here?"

'3 years' Maria's reply.

"Good!" do you like it here?"

"Yes"

"You will. I will give you some tips for beauty care. But I don't know how they remove those spots you have gotten. I think there might be some surgeries which can help. I will find out and let you know."

Nobody seems care for the time to night. They don't know how late they are tonight. Looks like they can talk, chat, gossip with coffee or wine all night. It's a nice break together amidst the busy routine of life. Maria felt like get up and go. Just at that moment Joseph came by the door of the room to look for her while at the same time veronica showed up too to check on Joseph said, 'oh, here you are! Looking for the family?" Joseph answered by holding Tito's hand 'yes, it's time to go home already very late." Veronica wondered instead of answering him "oh, Tito is here too! I thought Maria would bring him here from downstairs." and then looked at Tito to say, 'who you like most?

Mommy or daddy?" Tito looked at the lady blank and speechless. Joseph answer to do the courtesy "both. He likes both mom and dad."

"Very good! Veronica turns to Maria and Said "go get him dressed is very cold outside." "He's already dressed up'. Joseph replied on behalf of his wife. Veronica seemed very careful about the little and unnoticeable things said again, "oh really! I did not notice at all. Must be very tired." Both husband and wife looked at each other than at the host as she looked very tired and drowsy must be drunk also.

The party was not over yet. Maria and Joseph said "goodbye" and "good night's looked like to get rid of the party. They both proceeded by taking their son in hand towards the grand door of the way out. Maria looked back didn't know why might be to see the drunk and the rich foreign lady who was looking at them from behind by holding a part of the open big and wide front door to close over them with the very thirsty and drowsy eyes looked like the same as Mr. Brown's that evening. Veronica's Grand party that night put a question mark on her mind about the host's marriage in true sense.

3 years is not a long time but it is long enough to know a place, its culture and its nature. Maria and Joseph saw well enough of people's lives. Well enough of different people's different life styles and the different behaviors of life to different people under circumstances. Maria takes a look at her own life now. She is busy and happy in the current wave of busy life. People born in times in different lands to live. It's all about living. Every moment they Thrive is only to live may be only a few people like her question "why or for what"? She lived a life in a different way in a different land in the past in Wars, fears and uncertainties. Hope is still the day light which brought them here and it is still the "hope" guiding them through the struggle for betterment.

"Cultures" seem to be the costumes for different people living together here "life" is always the same? People are always people, men are men and women are all the women. In the mix and match of languages and cultures life flows still the same in terms of unchanged Human Nature. It always has its own way of existence as life goes with its own tricks despite times and lands. Global life moves on by setting rules, shaping or reshaping, playing tricks good or evil but all for fights and struggle simply to survive all in better scenario for the betterment and prosperity. According to the wise man life is the most precious gift which we don't want to lose. As a soldier we take oath on life but at the entrance of death we try hard to hold on to it. The most precious thing in life is life itself. Being alive is the urge for being well.

Time flies fast. Tito is school going now. Maria and Joseph live in a house in a better neighborhood. Maria goes to a job training center. Joseph found a better job in the cell phone company and earning a lot more money than before. Maria doesn't count every penny now. They go on vacations, visit different attractions in summer, and enjoy meals in good restaurants. They can share the aspects of present life even though it's a bit busier but okay to them as long they are moving forward.

Fall season now. Nature dressed in red and yellow. Little chill makes people feel nice and cozy in the warm clothes. Maria is walking ahead from the bus stop to Tito's school. By picking up from school she will go home she doesn't have time now-a-days to go to the park. Always busy at school and home. Thank God! Thought Maria" no complains about her little devil not even to hurry to pick him up from the office room. This is very common for being a mother of a restless and naughty early age School Boy. In the beginning Maria got suspicious about the teachers thinking they might not be fair to her son. Tito is doing well academically and the mother doesn't worry about her original nationality.

Nice neighborhood. Maria likes walking through the neighborhood garmented with the tall trees with green in summer and red- yellow in the fall against the nice set of nice houses. Sometimes the tall trees guard the houses by standing at the both sides or behind the houses. They cover a house from the front yard to beautify the home of a family with the blessings of Nature. Tito's talking Non-Stop as well as singing Rhymes while walking towards home by holding the dear moms hand. Exhausted and hungry mother is still enjoying the nice weather of fall season as between Extreme Hot and Cold. Tito continues hopping and singing in front of her suddenly spoke out 'I am hungry". Maria got surprised and asked 'why didn't you eat the lunch I gave you?'

'I ate but half of it. Teacher said that's too much. Mommy you are good you let me eat. Did you also have a mom mommy?'

'Yes of course, everyone has a mom. Mom's love children and teachers discipline them. Too much food at the school not good for the study and you don't want to be lazy and fat right?' Tito asked again 'will you cook Pasta for me tonight?' they all eat pasta and lasagna.'

'Don't you like rice and Curry anymore? How about pastry? I did not make pastries and Patty's long time.'

'You cook those a lot. I like new food.' joseph insisted and Maria nodded his head and said okay my boy I will make pasta for you.'

Most of the time Maria's company is her son only now a days. Joseph comes home late after having dinner outside. Doesn't matter anymore to her. He got busier what can she do? Still enough time to be with him at least in bed. Still a precious time to Maria a short time of togetherness as a couple in the bed at night by finishing a long day of work and struggle. She never complain about anything. Maria contacts Joseph's all relatives and friends in free time. She knows about their matters more than Joseph. She invites them, takes their invitations for weekends. But still she is less valuable when they meet. Seems like she is the media for the arrangements of meeting their friend joseph or cousin Joseph what so ever. Doesn't Know why Maria always notice women's status in the society, in the family actually Everywhere. They are not dominated by only men they are dominated by the same category previously suffered or still suffering.

She did not call anybody today Bilqees one of Joseph's friends wife called her after she finished helping Tito with his homework and dinner together.

'Hello, Maria? Did you hear the news about Sophia?' Bilqees seems very excited.

'no, why?' what happened to her?'

'Nothing happened. I just heard from Sophia that her husband is cheating on her. She was crying over the phone.'

'How did she know? What happened?'

'He went out for lunch with the lady colleague.'

How did she know?

'Another colleague of her husband told her.'

'It could be a misunderstanding or a silly suspicions or even might be a lie of gossips. Tell Sophia to come down.' Maria seemed very wise.

'Okay my boss!' Then asked next 'I heard Brother Joseph got a promotion. Good for him! Did you guys celebrate?'

'Yes we went out that day.' answered Maria

'Oh!' Bilqees did not seem very happy asked again 'did Brother Joseph give you a gift on the occasion?'

'He wanted to but we did not have time to go shopping. Doesn't matter we had a good time together. A little good time together in a busy life is as precious as a nice gift what you think?' Maria liked to pinch Bilqees this time. After some more conversations Maria hung up the phone. She knows now Bilqees, will call more other ladies to spread out the news of Joseph's promotion as well as the ill of Sophia's husband.

Add in another fall few years later with Maria's two children in the car now Tito and a baby girl. Time's running very fast as the speedy Car in which they are all sitting now. Maria is heading towards a shopping mall. While driving cannot see the beauty of fall season. The speed of Life took away the Leisure to view and enjoy Nature. Time and place both on nurturing Maria and her family with full responsibility. Their lives got going Maria doesn't know for better or worse. They are achieving success in many ways living a current standard living, having good jobs, school, cars and the ability to drive the car as well as the life as whatever capabilities and responsibilities it takes. They can afford a lot of things house, car, vacations and many other aspects of a rich country life. In the busy life style are they losing something? Thinks Maria a lot of time. She feels like something is not right. Something is missing she doesn't know what. One thing for sure bothers her very much which is her husband's late arrival and short stay with the family. Otherwise both Maria and Joseph are similarly capable and responsible to maintain everything as they have everything to live and enjoy a contemporary life. What else can she expect thought Maria.

Taking a glance at the turning red and yellow leaves outside through the Windows of the car. Thought Maria the green youth of Nature comes back again later after fall and winter but not the green Youth of life ever again. Life process in decay the lost youth never comes back. The memories of their love, Joseph's commitments torment her now. She happens to be always wise and mature but still cannot resist her jealousy for Jessica Joseph's business Partner. She doesn't want to believe in what Bilqees thinks about Joseph and Jessica and their togetherness doesn't matter if it is only for business. She cannot resist herself from being so mean and suspicious when her dear Joseph talks about Jessica another woman in his life doesn't matter for what reason. Sometimes she pretends to be afraid of only the gossips concealing her fear of losing her husband. She knows Bilqees as well as her gossips. Joseph and Jessica's story must have been circulated already.

She wants her confusions and suspicions go way. Her husband still loves her comes for her to make her happy. Children and wife still his priority. Maria is in doubt or no doubt about Joseph this is true existing two parts of life work and family or workplace and home giving birth to two kinds of relationships for both men and women a life partner and a business partner. Sometimes the later one making a relationship for some people tends to be a boyfriend or a girlfriend. Would Maria and Joseph admit themselves to the current trend? Definitely not their culture and strong family bondage don't give place to such an inconvenience. But how about the flow of the heart? Is complicated people still can't Define love when the love thing is a big issue between a man and a woman. Sometimes it looks like to her that achievements of concretes are associated with the achievement of the heart. But it still lies to believe that a broken heart man and man with a broken leg slow down the speed of life with whatever achievement or flourishment they desire. The change of the culture and one's own heritage shapes and reshapes human lives as the wind and waves form rocks. Heart follows its own choice and flows in it's own way.

Whatever, time is flying as usual. Maria and Joseph are still happily married living as a family with the progress of so-called better living in the contrary to their past life in their own land. Their community is also expanding with all hopes and gains, with all struggles through the ways of success and failure in happiness and distress. Business and gossips are also going with the flow of life. They all do a lot of new things to compete with one another. As they all mixed up in free mixing at work, business all in Social meetings a lot of interesting stories are being made up for Bilqees's keys to gossip and she is very busy and happy to circulate them around. Walking in the dark is nicer than the living with a Suspicious Mind in the bright daylight. Maria hates to be tormented and confused by Bilqees's stories and gossips. Her Suspicious Mind keeps her away from her happiness as well as from her love for her beloved. And a woman like Bilqees can only makes the air cloudy. She hates her sometimes while very inside she also needs her to find the unknown.

Today is a special day it's their 10th anniversary. They both are very happy and excited today and also very lucky to have this day on a week-end. Nothing can stop them to celebrate the day. They made plans. Joseph booked four seats in an expensive restaurant for the evening. He also bought an expensive dress for Maria and did not let her buy anything for him said "you are my best gift from life and you already gave me two precious gifts'.

'Two precious gifts?' Maria lifted her eyes up to wonder and joseph got naughty at once to keep her curiosity longer. He became playful and joking said 'I'll tell you later what they are' with a twist of two eye brows and a little wicked smile in the corner of his two closed lips.

In the nice summer morning of this special day Maria feels herself very refreshed as the cloud of a bad feelings from the last fight with Joseph over something disappeared to clear her sky. Having a good night with her husband made her cheerful and more energetic. She feels the nice day break in the backyard with a smile in her face. Rest of her family is still sleeping in bed. She has to do some household work and make some nice breakfast in the special morning. She feels herself successful in making a happy family. Yes! They are happily married. But still a little afraid because she doesn't know whether joseph will get a call from his work as he gets sometimes.

It's a nice summer anniversary like the summer day of their wedding ten years ago. If it takes three decades of their marriage till death this one would be the spring of their marriage. The fall and the winter are ahead. She is afraid to think of the fall as the fall of their marriage and the winter to be end. Not a lot of people here die with holding onto only one marriage or happily married till death.

She served breakfast with special care. Joseph is also happy and playful with children. Maria shared a good time by watching TV and playing video games but still again with a tension inside hoping to be free of it after 12 pm. if nobody means Jessica comes to pick joseph up for some business.

Maria and joseph skipped lunch for dinner in the evening. They spent time in the bedroom most like a newly married couple by sharing all good memories of their marriage. Leaning on the pillow said Maria

'I think I know what the precious gifts I gave you.'

'Good.' Answered joseph adding 'and I have a very special gift for you for today.'

Maria jumped with excitement 'really!' what is it? What have you got for me? Show me show me '. She jumped to sit on the pillow by folding two knees.

'Open the drawer.' Joseph's sweet command.

With a lot of excitement she opened the drawer and cried like a teen age girl 'aww!' when could not open the drawer.

'Come close to me I am giving it to you.' Joseph took her in his arms to take out the valuable gift hidden under the pillow. It's a small jewellery box looked like a ring in it.

'Do you know what is in it? Asked joseph playing naughty.

'I know it's a ring. What else.' Maria doesn't want to wonder.

'Just only a ring?'

'What is it then?'

'Ok, give me your finger.'

'But I have my wedding ring on.'

'Take that off! Then put this one on!'

'A diamond ring! Her joy knows no bound.

'Yes silly, it's a diamond ring. Do you know how much carat is the diamond?

'I don't care. It's a diamond therefore expensive. Valuable gifts for valuable person. I am valuable.'

'yes my love! You are worth of all the wealth I possess.

Joseph hugged her with a deep kiss. Maria never ever got so much happy in her life. She started looking at the finger wearing the gorgeous ring stretching to her eyes and also to the mirror. She felt herself so glorified with love and happiness in the land of opportunities.

5 pm. everyone dressed up to go out. Joseph in his new black suit, Maria in a gorgeous new black dress with outstanding embroidery. She is gifted today on her anniversary with a precious gift from her love. Children are looking very cute too. 'Nice family'! What else we need?' Thought Maria coming out of the house.

It's nice outside the door in the nice summer evening. Maria feels romantic in the nice summer breeze. She looked in the eyes of her beloved husband seeking for the same look she got at the blessed moment. But he seemed got busy to hurry to get in the car. Just at the very moment when Maria and Joseph looked at each other with so much love and cherishing memories Jessica's car arrived at the same spot with a cruel break of reality.

All the colors of a rainbow from Marias sky disappeared so quickly to cover with the cloudy cloud. She knows after talking with Jessica Joseph will come back only with a bad news a news of departure from the platform of love, hope and desire and a long time longing for a plan like this for them as a family. She knew Jessica didn't come without any reason. Her fear of losing the day didn't go wrong after all. Joseph came back with a pale face and a serious mood said that he has to go with Jessica for an urgent meeting as something went wrong suddenly in business. Maria doesn't care she doesn't want to know anything about their business all she cares now is Jessica's beauty and style as if seeing both herself and her rival in the same mirror. She didn't even hear what her dear husband said to say 'good by' or to apologise to leave. She looked ahead taking off her vision from the nice neighbourhood in the nice green summer evening. Her eyes kept gazing at Joseph beside another beautiful lady in an expensive car on her anniversary. She took off her eyes then to look at her expensive anniversary gift a 'diamond ring!' she felt herself like Veronica in a black gorgeous evening dress with all expensive ornaments. Her eyes became drowsy might also be looking like the rich lady Veronica at the end of her grand Christmas party. By looking back at rich lady she looked ahead to see Tito and the little precious Rose. They are the real gifts of her marriage. Now she knows the precious gifts of her marriage. They are the precious gifts ever to each other but alone with one parent cannot make the real sense of holy matrimony.

Story 2

CATHY AND THE KITTY

Friday morning. Chris is up in a very good mood as the early spring wind blew on his face soft and soothing as if his cute kitty touching him with its nice and soft fur. Friday! Yes!' the sweet eve of the week-end break. A free time after a five day busy and fussy long working days. Thinks Chris yawning and stretching 'time to leave the bed' fresh and not drowsy. He will have a cup of coffee with the touch of his only company in the small apartment or compartment in a very high rise building in the very modern and busy city and play with it his lovely and favourite kitty. It gives him a little luxury in his rush hours in morning time necessities of brushing teeth, bathing, dressing up quickly, and making breakfast in time and so on. Little kitty is always a little break for Chris in his busy and crazy life and a company in his loneliness. As right now she is meowing, rubbing herself on his feet, asking to be patted and fed by her master with a continuing look of all innocence in her eyes. How can anyone ignore that look of demand or need from the very pretty object like the kitty his one and only company in his lonely life. Chris always feels himself refreshed and ready for work by getting his little companions love and touch to leave the nice and cosy apartment up in the city sky.

The typing and handling papers is not hard or tough anymore but very boring and suffocating among many others in the office compartment. He himself and all others seem like some sitting objects facing the computers to comply with it. All of them look like dying every noon for the lunch break. Cathy calls him sometimes in the middle of his work to have a little chat over the phone a sweet little sin can't be resisted by any young man like Chris.

Lunch time. Finally! Walking in the busy street towards his favourite restaurant still a bit of fun by passing many beautiful girls with different complexions and beauty in different shapes, dresses and make-up. Some of them look moody while some look happy and cheering with some company. Some also look pale, bored and tired while again some might be angry and upset at something in the regular crowd. Still it's a break from work with a slight blow of a fresh air in the overwhelmed everyday crowed in the street.

The restaurant is nice and cosy. He often comes here sometimes also with Cathy. She likes their veggie dishes. He feels an emptiness whenever he comes alone. He pines for her non-stop talk, loud laughter, and her sweet smile every now and then between their conversations while walking together. Thinking of her took Chris to the old memories the memory of their first meeting in a fight and consequently their falling in love with each other and make friends. He smiled alone by thinking of his present girlfriend in a minivan loaded with all her goods to move to a new place which apparently by incident or co-incident got hit by Chris's car to bring these two strangers in love and a relationship led by a terrible fight. The loud and angry Cathy was very desperate to get herself into an enormous encounter on her part and a careless silly mistake on Chris's which was very annoying at first and lovely later as consequently built a relationship with a beautiful girl like Cathy.

The very moments ago desperate Cathy got on him shouting loud "have you lost your mind? Or don't even care about people! Do you know how much I have been trying to get things done? Selfish people! Fly in the air--------what is it? Careless dreamer! Flying in a sports car? Huh!'

Looking at the pretty young lady with a rose lips and two red fiery cheeks spitting out balls of fiery words towards Chris until he became very guilty and self-protective at the same time said with an apology 'sorry, it was just an accident. I'll pay for your loss. My car got damaged too.'

Cathy was still upset and loud expressing "how about my day? Do you have any idea how hard I was working?' she remained very demanding and didn't know at that moment that she was disclosing her heart to a stranger a very handsome young man as she was a beautiful young lady to fall in love eventually to make a relationship as a young couple in a very short period of time.

Some incidents bring people together to make friends. Bring two strangers close to each other into a relationship without any preparation and rethought. It just happens. Even though Cathy was still upset and quarrelsome did not think of calling the police for the incident or for the damage caused by the very stranger who happens to be her very dear present boyfriend playing a very important role in her life. In contrary she took all the help offered by the man named Chris from the street to her new home. Two opposite sex strangers made friends at once and set up a new apartment belonged to the opponent party in the accident on the road to make it a meaningful incident in their life.

It was a year ago. Even now Chris is thinking of her that fiery face with all her demands and blames. Still she lives there in the same apartment half an hour away from Chris's. The collision and the help of Chris brought two hearts together into a bondage of love and partnership a real relationship.

It was a year ago. Chris remembered her angry face now at this moment when she is not with him. They love each other to make a regular couple and planning to live together. It's been six months he is fighting with his parents to live with his girlfriend together in his apartment. It's not very unusual to have a girlfriend but the fact is Chris's parents do not live in the same city to watch over their son. The mom is very suspicious about the girls around normally happens to think like every other mom that her only precious son in the whole world would be taken away from her to make her bosom empty forever. The mom is very afraid to lose her control over her only son to another woman whom she doesn't know at all. Mrs. Williams doubt is baseless Cathy won't be able to make herself a suitable life partner for Chris as usually expected by in-laws family, social status, and fortune unfortunately. She lives alone as left her only one parent her mother long time ago who happens to be living with her second husband. Cathy never ever going to see her again as promised for some reason. It was then when she moved to her new place all alone with all of her furniture as met Chris to fight and love to live together eventually after.

Few days' later mom got very upset and eventually helpless when Chris brought the jobless Cathy home in his own apartment. Suddenly she lost her job and apartment both to the situation to make the would be mother in law much more worried about not only the trouble but also a huge burden on her son's shoulder.

It's a phase of time which is a part of two young boy and girls' life in today's world. One has lost her job residing with the other has a job. One is spending the whole time searching for a job another is busy working at work place out of home. The kitty is in between doesn't know the hardship of life used to be lonely when Chris was not at home. Now better having the company of Cathy when she is around.

No job interviews today for Cathy staying home since morning. The cat is playing around her sometimes comes closer to get some attention, love and care, purring to be patted or sleeping at ease with full security and comfort. All these to be done by Chris now by both. Cathy took some responsibilities for both her boyfriend and his pet. They look like parenting the pet together.

Its noon time. Cathy is still busy at the computer applying for a job. She went through eleven job interviews so far. Still no luck. The bank account is almost going to be empty. She needs to go out to do some shopping for some necessary things. Feeling helpless at this point. Asking for money from her partner doesn't seem just. Chris has done already a lot for her and now she is staying free at his place and also sharing the dinners he brings home or orders at restaurants.

She thought for a moment by looking at the kitty 'does she feel the same way? May be not. It's just an animal to be grateful to its master for food, shelter and care.

She left the computer desk and opened the curtains to look outside through the windows. Wide glass windows, the open sky, the green of the parks and places, the soothing breath of God are all behind the glasses. She can put a hand on the glass but cannot touch the green or feel the open air and the sky. Inside behind the barriers of crystal clear glasses is the cool of air-conditioning which is keeping the kitty and herself alive. Yes, alive by means of money only. Everything is purchased with money. A nice small apartment is affordable by Chris only one more person can share which is now Cathy. Luckily the bed is double to share. Cathy put all her furniture in a storage and sharing all of Chris's. The T.V. the computer and the bed has only one soul to share unlike the chairs, table, desk and so. This is called human heart which is allowing two people to live together after all.

Three weeks gone no job yet. Only the job search drives her browsing through her brain nowadays. She just left the computer desk by finishing up some job applications for a cup of coffee. Had the breakfast with Chris before he left. Chris promised to bring Chinese for dinner tonight. Cathy doesn't say her choice even though asked by him. She thinks wired now a days as questioning herself 'do people feed on each other?' is she a cannibal? Is she worthless surviving on her boyfriend? What if her boyfriend was not there for her at her time?' she is very grateful and down at the same time. Chris likes to enjoy the time with her but Cathy can't really help herself much to comply with him.

All in a sudden between her thoughts the phone rang and the kitty jumped in her lap with a loud meow by giving Cathy a little shock to hear and fear for a movement. She got up and picked up the phone with hope and fear at the same time. Hope for a good news for getting a job and fear to be disappointed. Kitty was watching her all the time while she was on the phone with cat curiosity and wonder and jumped back down when the new master put the phone down. Cathy blushed with a sudden happiness and excitement. A sparkle of warm sun shine peeped through the glass-window to spark through her heart. She jumped up with a cheer to lift up the kitty again to hug with all the comfort of her heart. Finally! Finally she got a job after so much of frustrations and anxiety.

Another Friday morning for Chris. This time with his lovely girlfriend. He is cheerful as always with a spirit of a Fridays approach to the up-coming week-end. Cathy's still sleeping while he started to browse his fingers on her soft naked back facing towards him in bed a very nice and soft body very beautiful to look and touch at the same time. He likes her nice and soft body as always. Knowing him awake the cat came in and jumped up to reach its masters and sat right beside Chris. Cathy woke up too while her boyfriend's hands were touching most parts of her sexy body. She rubbed her eyes and joked 'kitty is beside you. Who will you like to pat now?' Chris twisted his eyes to say 'you are my kitty I will pat you!' by putting his hands and fingers again on her said 'look! So soft and warm just like my kitty. I want to lie a little more by hugging you.' As approached to hug her the cat meowed to remind him the morning. 'Oh! Still a working day. Let's get up. Chris picked up the cat walked towards the bathroom patting it. Cathy will do the same in a few minutes and they both will be busy and ready for work. By having breakfast themselves and by feeding and patting the cat also they will leave the apartment by leaving the kitty inside by locking up the door of the previous part of their conjugal life to come back again by the end of the day for the remaining part.

Friday night after work. Having dinner together with a friend Chris and Cathy came to a club for dance and friends as usual. After midnight they got tired of dancing a bit drunk too to get out of that place for a fresh air with their best friend Sam. He is actually Chris's childhood friend now very close to Cathy also.

They started walking in the quiet dark city street lighted by the lights of big displays up, the lights of the night clubs, restaurants, hotels or closed shopping centres with their bright and lighted big banners. Nowhere to go now at this hour. So they started heading towards the bridge by passing Radom night girls, some crazy honks and loud squeaky scratch of the drunk drivers of the night.

Not many people around on the bridge. They stopped by the high railings on the bridge on the lake. The water seems very still with no movement at all seems like waiting for commands above to rise too high or low waves with the rhythm of the blow of the cold wind. Chris and Sam talking non-stop about business, politics, current economy and so on. Cathy is enjoying the warm fall's nice cool breeze blowing her hair with a gentle touch. A little tiny thin bunch of hair falling again and again on her fore-head little down to her eyes to keep her busy to remove it again and again. It is also nice to look up in the sky and down at the water. Watching her looking at the sky Sam came forward to say 'look at the sky. Too crowded by stars looks like night guards as each and every one is a lamp to watch us down on the ground.

'People don't think that way. I didn't know that you are also a poet along with all of your philosophy. By the way how is your writing going?'

'Good! I am good. Writing, working, enjoying life at the same time. It's good to have a friend like Chris.

How about you? Is Chris being a good boy?'

'Chris? You mean he is cheating on me or not?'

'Of course not! What you think? I'll kill him if he hurt you a bit. Don't worry life is good keep going with love and company in the course of life.'

'Thank you for a good advice. Such an honorable friend!' they both laughed loud at her last words.

Watching Chris smoking alone Cathy got a bit absent minded looking at the sky again calm and quiet. By noticing her mood Sam said again 'beautiful stars!

'yes!' answered Cathy a little absent minded then added more to a story 'did you hear the story they say to children that the closest persons people love become stars in the sky after they die?' looking at Cathy's sad and pale face answered Sam "may be the story came down to console little children at the loss of their parents or so'. Looking at her said Sam again 'people live with the loss and move forward come on silly girl!'

Cathy changed the subject matter now pretended to be a lot more mature one to ask 'never mind! What were you guys talking about? Politics? Business? Or wars may be?'

'Yes, of course! We care about the world. And you girls are chicken! Care about your small world fashion, beauty, shopping, friends, love and care.'

'It's not small it's all necessary leading you guys to the big world. Small worlds make a big world. For instance, love and care help people grow and live healthy. And the money and women you men care about giving the business to your big world to get going by shopping, fashion and beauty care. Woman's products sale the most in the market. What you think man?'

'That's true'. Said Sam 'we share the world, rule the world together with love and care and all.'

Chris came close to them and asked 'what are you guys talking about? Looks like having a debate.'

"It's over. You missed the fun.' Chris urged to know by showing a fake suspicion 'what is it! Don't even think of making a move on my girl!' answered Sam pointing at Cathy 'ask her. She knows.' Cathy brought everyone back to the fact said 'cut it out! It's getting late. We need to go home now'. They started walking back to the cars to leave a nice late Fall night behind not knowing another night like that will ever come back again with friends and lover.

Nice evening. The ravine outside looks beautiful through the glass doors. The trees are alarming the departure of fall in yellow and red. Cathy intended to go out of the room to the balcony to take some pictures of nice colors in Nature's beauty a full beauty of the fall before it turns into winter. She got up to take the camera but just at that moment the phone rang to give her a real alarm

'Hallow'! Cathy's voice.

'Hi! Is this my sons place?' a female voice most likely an elder.

'Who you looking for? Who is your son?'

'I am sorry, is this Chris's residence? The other party got shy.

'Yes it is. Who is calling? Asked Cathy with proper courtesy.

'I am his mother. Who are you?' other party got rude from an apology very instantly.

'I am his friend.' Cathy answered by thinking a bit not to disclose herself yet.

'Where is Chris? And what are you doing in my sons place?

'I just came by to deliver some important documents. He is not home I guess will be arriving soon.'

'Tell him that I called his mom and also please inform him that I am along with his dad is in town thank you.'

Chris's parents chose to stay in a hotel as their son got only one bed room. When they came to see him Cathy stayed out and Chris worked real hard to wipe out all her signs in the apartment except her clothing. Finally he managed that too. Mom shouldn't find out his relation with a girl whom she doesn't know. Chris was very excited to show his nice little apartment to his mom a little but an achievement in his life so far yet. It's his own therefore have some value to show to his parents. Mother jane watched every single thing around with care also with an intention to find some clue for things 'not right' or not properly 'organized' or broken, ugly or torn. She opened every drawer, put things from here to there, re-organized the kitchen and so on. His parents loved the kitty and patted her too.

At the dinner parents asked Chris every possible questions about his wellbeing to make sure that their son is O.K., healthy as well as wealthy as a young man should be. Since they came to visit him they have been discussing a matter among themselves something looks important might be a current issue needs to be solved. Chris tried to guess. It should be about him his job or his marriage. Mothers are always worried about their beloved sons to be snatched away by a witch along with all of their fortune. From their whispering, their remarks at the dining table about his life style Chris managed to guess right it must be his marriage. The next moment he got very lucky to be over heard their conversation on his marriage.

'She is beautiful and intelligent used to be his friend when they both were little' mothers concern. Father William said, 'o, yes. They knew each other since their childhood till they entered high school. Mr. and Mrs. Frank are good people. Their only daughter would be the only heir to their wealth and businesses.'

'Oh! Right! It would be a perfect match. I know they liked each other. Let me ask Chris if he still remembers her.' Said mom Jane.

So its money and marriage together' thought Chris but couldn't figure out which girl they are talking about. Mother got him after a few minutes and asked 'do you remember Nancy?'

'Which Nancy?'

'The one was in our neighbourhood in our old place remember? Both of you were little. It was your childhood''.

Chris didn't take much time answered promptly 'I remember her!' as if he did not hear them. And also pretended that didn't think about Cathy his present girlfriend.

'We are going to visit them. Mr. Frank invited your father and me to visit their place. They are still living at the same place. Have flourished a lot I heard from our friends. Do you want to see Nancy? We can travel together'.

'I love to but let me check my vacation and holidays.'

'Let us know sooner. We love to be with you for some time.'

Cathy is staying alone in the apartment as Chris is out with his parents heading towards another state. He did not tell her about his parent's intention. He doesn't want to hurt her or to be worried. He himself is not in a mood to marry right now. He only wanted to see his childhood friend only to please his parents and also wanted to have some time spent with his parents somewhere as they wished too. A little bit longer time with parents in their old place would be nice with all the childhood memories. It's a kind of feeling romance in the memory of childhood through high school, in the memory of the old place where he grew up in a distinct neighbourhood with some lovely companions at the very lovely and early age in a lovely place far and far away in another state once was very close to heart. While he remembered his early age in his old lovely place he remembered his old friendship and his friend Nancy once was his very close friend. Now while his parents are thinking and planning about Nancy to be his life partner. Cathy is already here as his best partner. They live together, share things together without talking or thinking about love. All Chris know is that he loves her company. They are living a time together doesn't want to think deep. Chris is better off now with Cathy whether mom likes it or not. His life is his life. It should be his own choice to decide who he choose for his life partner as in marriage of which parents always think about.

A few changes have been noticed about the city by Chris as he reached the destination. The city they left long time ago looks older but not that much. Some new developments have been noticed and some old parts of it look older almost to perish. Random developments of big mansions, houses, community centres and schools and parks make the residential areas sophisticated, nicer looking with a new look. They all wanted to see their old home in the old neighbourhood.

Busy life and busy life style consumed all the childhood memories to present a new one. Chris started to wonder about how could he remained to live all these years without cherishing the memories of his own childhood and the places with the people he grew with his mom and dad; his young age friends; his school; his classmates from kindergarten to high school. If his parents wouldn't have taken an attempt to come here he wouldn't have a chance to look back. How could he be so thoughtless and also heartless! He wonders now by thinking how the struggle through the busy life style made him such a looser. He has been browsing the icon throughout the computer screen not throughout his sweetest memories.

Nancy! The playmate, the sweet girlfriend up to high school! How his life beyond this old neighbourhood did not let him have a space to think of her or to cherish the past in his memories? Ever since they moved from the place Chris and Nancy contacted each other only e few times in the beginning. Both of them could not even got a bit nostalgic in the speed of busy life after to stop for some time to think and to look back.

Still 15 min. to go for Nancy's house. Mom is talking non-stop in the car mainly about Nancy. And Chris knows why. She has been trying to give him the memories of her nature, her beauty and her friendship with him. As she going like 'do you remember our old house? We had a nice backyard. You and Nancy used to play there with all other children. You had a swing and she liked to swing a lot. She was so cute! I loved her like a mother and she was very attached to me. She was a cutie used to say 'aunty, I like brownies' and I would say 'o, yeah I made brownies yesterday and I still have some left for you'. Or 'I know you love brownies I'll make some this evening only for you!' in order to catch sons attention to the attempt to impress him by her intended future daughter-in law she also added these impressive words with some emphasis 'you know sometimes some relationships are called heart-relationship same as the existing blood relationship.

By looking very deeply into Chris's eyes continuing the talk like 'you two were a perfect play-mates together. I loved to see you both together a lot. You two played together, fought together without any harm ever. Fight and friendship you know which one wins over another?' Chris did not listen to all of what was said but now suddenly looked at the wise mother over all her silly womanly attempts to impress him answered shortly 'friendship mom!' mother jane's eyes cheered with an unknown non-spoken smile to utter the cheerful and happy word a little single word 'yes'! And asked with a hope 'did you remember those days?'

'Not much but have come to remember now.'

Mrs. William got surprised said 'no! You don't remember old days? Didn't even think of Nancy? Why what's wrong with you guys?'

'I have been busy. We have to go through tough struggles to keep us up with the speed of life now. Memories are memories just don't have enough to think about. I am thinking now memories come back. When I' see her today I'll recall old Nancy with all of the past. 'O yes! You will be glad to see her. She is very attractive. Mrs. Howard showed me a photo of her when we met the Howard couple last year. Since then we have been making a plan to visit the lovely family in our memorable old town.

Chris knows by now what makes a family lovely. Big house, social status, or money and future. Everyone in our society is struggling to have a position in the society. A young man like Chris goes with a goal-set for future along with a life or a youth to cherish with love and company, with friends and families to live or cherish a life while struggling to achieve a good career for the betterment of the present and of the future. Usually a few of the young generations think of the future in this current time. Most of them like to live with comfort and to enjoy the life most. Chris has not reached the time yet to think about prestige, status, future and fortune or even power to keep himself up. They live for being alive only do things whatever it takes. Education, jobs, trainings, values, a heart full of desires associated with the body while they keep going with the flow where there is not much to think. Cathy is his love and company now didn't think about marriage or children yet. May be then he'll have the maturity to think about raising a fortune for future.

They all got very surprised and impressed by the big new mansion of Mr., and Mrs. Frank when they reached there. Mother Jane whispered into her sons ears 'do you see! Wow! I can't believe! They have a house like this now! Wow! O! Wow!' Chris hushed his mom and stepped forward. While entering the big hallway through the huge doors opened by Mrs. frank Mrs. Jane started looking around at all of the decorations. Looking up at the big gorgeous chandelier. Mrs. frank seems enjoying Mrs. Williams wonder at their achievements. Good to show.

After all the 'hi and hello's Mr. William commented frankly by looking at Mr.Frank 'Nice!' very big house. How big is the house? How many rooms?'

Mr. Frank got very courteous said 'I----will show you the house this, this way let's have a sit.' And by taking a sit on the gorgeous sofa in the very specious living room added 'after so long two families are getting together. By noticing Nancy's absence said again addressing his wife 'where is Nancy?'

'She is coming. Just finishing up something. She'll be here any moment'.

Chris took his sit in front of two fathers and kept silent to listen to their conversations. Very slowly he dipped into his thoughts. Doesn't know how to feel about the getting together. Nancy's parents seem as friendly and easy as old days but he doesn't know about his parents. He himself feels an unknown barrier between these two families at this moment. So far he recalls his old days when they were at the same level. Both families had same kind of houses and same status. But now the same other family seems belong to a different category according to the build-up social structure which is apparently high up. Two families now standing on two uneven levels not good for getting along.

Nancy was already there while he was judging himself at the big house of hers. When opened his eyes saw a very simple young woman in loose casual pants and shirt. No makeup, no hair done. Beautiful or not but the face out of a very thick forehead covering by hair seems very familiar 'how are you Chris?' Chris seemed to be woke up one more time to recall not the voice only but the way she was throwing those words towards her old friend. Very long ago someone used to ask 'how are you?' usually when he lost a game to her while playing together. This simple and a common question of 'how are you?' used to be a hurt for Chris while asked by Nancy very naughty with the naughty twist of her eyes. This is not the same kind of moment but still Chris doesn't know why it hurts a bit in the new environment of a rich set –up all around. His parents are watching every detail of their big house inside and out asking questions about the materials used to build the house or the size and square feet's. While Mr. and Mrs. William were wondering at the sophistications and glory of the house with all the expensive materials used garnet, marble, paintings, high ceilings, nice decorations and the designs. Chris started to wonder at the people of the house as how and why they are still the same, friendly and simple without any pride or vanity. Still it is different feel now for both Chris and Nancy. It is different for the long gap of time for both of them but for Chris it is also Nancy's present status. They cannot feel themselves as friendly as before.

Sitting by the nice indoor pool from where they can view the beautiful and well-maintained garden they took the first chance to know about each other after so long time. They were a boy and a girl then but now they both are young a pretty young woman and a handsome young man.

Chris opened his mouth first to ask 'what are you doing now-a-days Nancy?'

'I am a fashion designer.'

Did you design any of the decorations of your house?'

'How do you know? I designed the drapery, some wall papers, chose the paintings of some parts and a little of the home decorations.'

'See! I knew it!' a spark of old friendship showed up in these words of Chris as if like of the boyhood. Nancy smiled too the early friendship smiled in new days. Then asked 'how about you? How is life?'

'Well, busy working as a clerk living in a little condo and apart from parents unlike you.'

'Also must have a girlfriend enjoying life a bit right?' Chris avoided the answer asked instead 'why you don't have a boyfriend?'

Nancy also took the different way to continue the conversation or to get rid of the curiosity to know each other's personal life said 'life is busy and different in your city. Here we are a little different partially rural still a bit conservative as living in the family.' Then thought a bit and asked again 'is Aunt Jane is a bit worried about you?'

Chris got annoyed and answered with hesitations 'why? Why? You think like that? Are you trying to be my guardian?' they both laughed together now to become friends again most probably. Chris took a look again at the riches of Frank family. He put more attention to the well decorated and gorgeous big house from the lovely and prestigious swimming pool. The tall marble pillars and the tall spiral staircases are showing its aristocracy with the height of the level of status were Nancy is standing now. bringing back his close and keen observations of his childhood friends new house apparently his moms major concern along with all of Nancy's parents present wealth and status asked Chris 'don't you think it's a big and huge house in the neighbourhood to stand alone?' 'Who cares? Who grows before who? We still live solitary not much or fast competition yet.

Chris knows his mom is watching him with Nancy where ever in the house with a hope of their upcoming relation. Chris took a look at the house and then at Nancy. Thinking Chris now this kind of house is desirable but not by marrying someone like Nancy or anybody else to get riches like that. He has good taste but doesn't aspire to reach the levels of high up by giving up his true feeling and freedom. He goes his way. He desires and achieves with his hard work. He believes to build up his own fortune by his own efforts.

Looking at Nancy he remembered Cathy's face and her lovely company. He loves his life with a freedom, some comfort, with some friends and a partner like Cathy to cherish a life in youth. He doesn't like to be bothered by the complicacies of a social life or social status or the complicacies of family relations. Our Chris doesn't want to purchase a wealthy bondage in exchange of his freedom.

Leaving the old city and the old refined memories behind Chris along with his family is back in the car. Mom and dad are still talking about the progress of Frank family. Looking at the mom, his ever innocent mom always pining for all the good for her only child may be one day he will be a parent looking ahead for achievements of his children or a child as the success of his own failure. Do all the parents like to set the goals for their children according to their unachieved success? Poor parents! Hard working parents wished so much by sending him to school, by saving every penny earned by their clerical job in order to get a better future for their only son by perishing only a little portion of their lives. Their hopes and desires combined got focused on the betterment of their son Chris. But still he doesn't want to believe in the M' words money and marriage and hates to think of wife and wealth. He doesn't want to lose the values which mom and dad are going to lose in order to get what they could not get by means of all the values and hard work. Dignity and freedom are most precious gifts of life. He doesn't blame his parents. Sometimes people slip over 'pain and gain' in life while they don't compensate with each other in true sense.

Ironically coming back to the regular life also seemed a little unfamiliar to him on the first day. Cathy's warm welcome with lots of hugs and kisses did not turn him as before. Cathy was very passionate not Chris. Cathy cooked dinner with a hidden desire in a hidden night costume hidden in her closet of clothing with the desires of the heart. Chris came back from the shower by finishing his shaving and shower to appear at the dinner table. He looked at the chair awaiting him to be sited not at the girlfriend awaited to be appreciated with love and care.

Unlikely but still likely Nancy's first question 'how are you?' came out of Cathy's mouth like 'how was your trip?' seemed startled Chris asked suddenly and he lifted his eyes towards Cathy with a question mark in his mind not in his eyes said 'good! It was nice to see old people and old city with parents. Ah! After so long I got to together with my parents. Do you know I met my childhood friend Nancy there? So much change after long time!'

Cathy started joking 'did you feel the old love for your friend or you would say 'she is just my childhood friend.'

'Don't worry. She is not you. You are my lovely kitty.' The cat meowed at the same time and Chris jumped over to pick it up with so much fun. The kitty started purring and Chris started to pat. Cathy started eating without asking anymore questions while looking at the kitty's comfort in the lovely touch of its human lover.

Saturday morning. Cathy and Chris supposed to sleep longer in the morning. Well, Chris is sleeping not Cathy. She is trying to read woman's magazine can't really concentrate. She is just going over the headlines like 'tips for to get a good night sleep', 'best week-end plans', or 'love and lovers' etc. the kitty behind the door meowing a little not loud. It knows the master is sleeping.

Finally, about at 10.00 am Chris is forced to wake up by his mom's phone call. Cathy doesn't want to be sneaky in the middle of their conversation. She got up and took the cat with her to the dining room.

Mom is very curious to know whether he contacted Nancy by now.

'Did you call Nancy yet?'

'For what?'

'what you mean?' she is your childhood friend.'

'Keep her that way mom! Don't force me or her to your way. There is nothing between us.'

'I just want you to keep in touch with her. Don't you have a face book account? Why don't you invite her '. The mom still encouraging or insisting in a way. Chris got annoyed a bit said 'why Mom? Why are you doing this? I am not thinking about anything like marriage.'

Chris knows mom will do something to get the other party to contact him.

Days are passing with the routine. Cathy and Chris are still living together. Eating and sleeping together. Going to work together and coming back together well in the same car. Living in the same home or riding in the same car could not keep the bondage tight enough to keep a real relationship as a couple. The emotional attachment towards each other started getting less and less very slowly without making them aware of the difference in true sense. They are living together doing things together in the same busy routine of a city life style. They work, they go out, they sleep, and they eat with less talk. They even don't have some spare time to tease each other, to have some funny talk nor even give their relationship a space to have some conversations about current social, political or ethical issues from the core of the modern city life.

Chris's mom couldn't convince him to think about marrying Nancy but Nancy made it possible to change him. They both together are true friends now. Cathy didn't mind their relation. When she met her she seemed much matured and business minded. Nancy and Chris started sharing views mostly about business, sales, advertisements, etc. They don't see each other but they are connected all along by communications through Facebook, phone, and emails. Very slowly they built up a relationship which did not bother Cathy but loosened her relationship with her boyfriend without her knowledge. And when she realized it was already late enough to bring her old Chris back to her life together with him in the apartment and in bed; at breakfast, dinner and also sometimes at lunch together; in movies and theatre; in company with their other friends in all other aspects of life except their two different jobs of their own. A change in Chris started to bother her after almost a year. Whatever time they got together Chris talks about business about how to become rich. Through Nancy's connections he is getting the contracts of designer products and clients. He is busy on week-ends with important business meeting and dinners. Cathy spends her week-ends alone now-a-days. Sam and his philosophies are also gone from Chris's life.

Cathy has started feeling lonely and thoughtful about her relationship with Chris. In this life living with someone like Chris didn't leave anything for her except her love for him. The lack of his company hurts her, gives her pain in her heart. Two people can't live together without an emotional bondage. Some Saturdays he doesn't even come home at night. The answer of Chris like 'don't worry I am not sleeping with anybody'. Cathy tends to believe him but it hurts when he doesn't say these words anymore 'I like you. You are my kitty'.

Overseas Nancy and many other girls are around him but he doesn't seem to be in love with any one anymore. Was he ever in love with anybody? Cathy questions herself also 'was Cathy herself also ever in love with Chris?' she doesn't know but her pain, the pain for losing his company and his touch is telling her that she loves him.

Recently Chris's mom calling him a lot. She can guess from their conversation that Chris is arguing a lot about her. He told Cathy finally that mom knows about her now and also the fact that his friendship with Nancy is neutral and based on their business together only. He is not thinking about her. Cathy believes him and everything he says. She knows Chris who is true about his feelings. Actually he is honest about everything. Thinks Cathy 'is this honesty or cruelty?' she feels herself 'unnecessary' in his life now. Demands and ambitions changed him very slowly. May be Chris himself also doesn't know that he has been carried away by his hidden inner ambitions. The life they enjoyed together happy, playful, cosy with passions is no longer no more. The sharing and caring was human. Now the aspiring ambitions seem carried him away nowhere beyond Cathy's reach down below where she lives and pines like a kitty purring for a human touch.

Some more time has been passed very fast for Chris but very slow for Cathy. She is mostly alone in his apartment and the time she gets in his company is unbearable. He is either at the computer or on the phone arguing about her or talking with the clients as well as with Nancy. Cathy gets ashamed or guilty for her relation with Mrs. Williams son also for living in his apartment. To Cathy life is shameful and hard with no break or compensations with some fun, feelings and passion, a passion which conveys some love, likings and attractions towards each other in a relationship. Even if Chris would fight with her over their relationship against the son and mom relationship or could at least talk about the whole thing would have been a relief for her to live or to breathe with a hope in the dead silence in the boundary of a concrete structure.

She doesn't feel good at all about living at the same place with her so called boyfriend. She made up her mind to leave and to break up with Chris. Actually there is no more relationship to break up it's just a choice to leave 11.00 am in a cold Saturday morning. Two cold hearts in two cold bodies lying side by side just got up from a cold night sleep. Chris is playing on his smart phone and the other cold heart is looking outside the window. The falling cold white snow is dropping from the ever quiet-living sky. The huge boundary of earth opened up her vast bosom to consume everything falling from the sky with enormous tolerance. Cathy's unspoken pain is stuck inside where there is no base to drop down to empty the cage. She started thinking that Chris's feelings seem baseless which doesn't endure anything in contrary to hers. His heart feels to cherish things, to enjoy things, but not to possess anything good or bad to feel with pain or to lose or gain. He is ever happy keeps going just with a pause sometimes by fixing the irregularities or some obstacles on the way. He is therefore free and honest.

Cathy opened up her mouth first saying 'you don't want me anymore right?' instead of saying 'love me anymore'. Chris hesitated a bit then answered 'look, I don't mind you stay here with me. I'll talk with you about our relationship later some other time. Do not feel bad you are fine-----you are fine. It's just----------it's just------- I'll explain to you later----------

The phone rang as usual on a Saturday morning. It must be his mom. Cathy shut her mouth and started watching Chris continuing the conversations argumentative but assertive and assuring at the same time. The conversation took quiet long until finally he blew out by saying 'leave me alone! Mom! My life is my life--------'the opposite side hung up. Looking at Chris's burning red face Cathy shirked with enormous guilt. It's all because of her. With a fear inside she went close to him very slowly like the kitty does sometimes. She looked him in the eyes said 'look, I don't want to give you any more trouble. I can live by myself now. You have done enough for me it's time to say 'good bye'. Never mind I won't blame you for anything. You are a nice and an honest person.' Chris felt guilty himself too and came closer without a touch to say' Cathy, I like you a lot but I don't know how it happened that I couldn't build up a relationship with you. Don't think that I am in love with someone else or thinking of marrying someone. I just need some more time to reach my goal. Life doesn't end like this. You need to grow up also. Become something wrother for yourself and also for all. I am sorry, I'll do everything to help you.' Looking longer at his face and into his eyes Cathy nodded her head a bit to say only 'yes' very very slowly.

Eventually on the day of moving Chris couldn't help her at all. He had to go for a meeting but promised Cathy that he will come back so that she should wait for him for the final meeting and saying 'good bye' to each other for the last time according to Chris might be for temporary. But by now after so long of inconsistency Cathy knows in her heart that this will be the last seeing of each other.

She didn't have much stuffs to take. She did all the shifting comfortably. Her own furniture is waiting in the storage where she left at the time of moving into his apartment. Cathy knows Chris won't be able to come to move those too as he did before. Life has gotten busier she is getting busy too.

It's time for Chris to say 'good bye' to Cathy. Cathy has been waiting for one hour with a suitcase will go with her in the taxi. Chris kept his word and came back to do the courtesy at least. Also offered her to go together for a dinner before she leaves and Cathy's answer was a short one 'not today I am tired. But thanks!' Chris didn't insist but gave her a cold hug to say 'good by'. They wished all the best for each other for the rest of the life though. The kitty showed up at the same time though when Chris came forward to pick up Cathy's suitcase. The cat came running towards the open door. Chris got busy instantly to get the kitty instead in fear of losing it if it runs away. Cathy's suitcase remained on the porch as before. The heavy burden of all necessary belongings remained there for Cathy herself no one is left to pick it up for a bit of help. Chris had no choice but to say 'good bye' in short by holding the kitty into his arms. Cathy picked up her heavy suitcase by all means with a thin smile said 'it's ok'. I can go by myself. You take care.' And Chris also added final courtesy to the final 'good by' with these nice words 'be well. Wish you all the best'.

He stepped out, opened the taxi door for Cathy and kept standing there until the taxi started running with his ex-girlfriend. She looked outside the taxi window and waved her hand to her dear Chris and the kitty for the last time.

Cathy's still kept looking not at Chris but at the kitty in his bosom so calm, quiet, comfortable and very dearly loved. Cathy recalled again Chris's love words spoken often before in their past 'you are my kitty. I love you so much.' How can she forget those words, those soft touches, the touch of love may not to Chris but always to her.

Chris and kitty are out of sight now but can't be out of her mind. She tried to close her eyes at the very near past at the sight of love by looking at crossing green signals, to view greens of the roadside views. The taxi is speeding up towards the main street. It will speed up more after as merging with the speed of the highway traffic.

Story 3

MAIDS AND THE MISSES

'Miss? Hallow! ---hello miss!'

'Who? Is it you Lisa?'

'Mam?' someone's gentle touch woke me up. Drowsy I gazed at the air angel with the eyes open with enormous wonder.

'Can you fasten your seat belt please?' the airhostess smiled with so called courtesy and took attempt to help me out with the seat belt. I pulled myself together to get myself out the drowsy and hazy front view to do what needed to do at that moment fastening the seat belt a very simple but very important at the same time. Putting on the belt on the airplane while travelling on the air. We are descending 'we are landing!' I can't believe that I am almost there 'Bangladesh'! An unnoticeable but still noticeable tiny little spot on the map I don't know why I am so much excited. It's not like visiting a grand historic or very well developed, rich and therefore an upright country to visit with all the curiosity and greatness and wonder of the heart. It is simply Bangladesh a tiny place might have its own wonders while not noticeable at all with any kind of historic greatness or values of the progress of modernism or human civilization along the way. Perhaps my excitements, or interest to the little world is because of the greatness of a friendship. Yes, it is my friendship with my friend Shaun the Bengali classmate of my own and a co-worker back in U.S.A six years ago.

I feel myself very lucky to be invited by him to see him, his family, and his country. Apart from the pictures of flood, poverty and political crisis given by Medias I pictured Bangladesh in my imaginations by the stories told by Shaun his lovely memories of his childhood, his youth, his student life, his family bondage, his love, his excitements, his feelings for his culture costumes and his dear country. The way he sees things, feels things it's all about love and attachments. I would love to see all of his belongings as I love to taste all of his country's delicious food knowing that my views, my heart and my taste would see, feel and taste things differently but still I am very very interested in what he has gotten here. Since I imagined all through his views. No matter what he is my friend, a very good friend of mine and who knows I might like and taste things the way he and his people do?

The flight is downward while the lighted sight of the civilization is visible through the round and tiny windows. The beautiful view of the vast lighted city down on earth doesn't make any difference between the well-developed places of mine from where this flying object took off. The views of the bright city down from very above always the same at the moment of departure or arrival. The enchanted views don't make the difference from where was our departure and to where is our landing. Things look nice when we overlook. Let's see what experiences are awaiting there in Shaun's land.

It's 2 pm. When I am here in Dhaka airport proceeding forward with the smiles and assurance of the co- Bangladeshi American passengers with me. Couldn't see any person like me in the whole crowd while looked around inside the airport. Got also a bit of fear inside me, a fear of a very visible minor into the whole major populations especially when it's totally unknown. It's not a black sheep among the white it's a white one among the black literally browns. The fear was gone after getting an easy check-out with a lot of hospitality and honor at the same time. Bunch of boys most probably not from the very well-being class came forward to help me with the luggage as soon as I got of the exit. Pushing forward through the crowd one of the boy quickly picked up my suitcase without even asking me. By securing his catch after a few steps forward he looked back to me to ask only 'taxy?' as soon as I nodded to say 'no' he dropped down my suitcase and asked just like earlier 'dollar?' I looked at the poor boy may be doesn't know any more of a few words in English. Very quickly he snatched away the little money I gave him and left. Instead of looking for Shaun I was still looking at the boy of the visible poor community. Unexpectedly all in a sudden he stopped and looked back to me to say only 'thankyou' with a spirit of sudden happiness and joy in his smile and a greatness in his eyes by holding the unexpected big note for him for a little job.

Shaun approached from nowhere with a beautiful lady happens to be his wife. I have seen her photos did not realize that his wife is this much beautiful. They received me with the courtesies with all their hearts. Shaun is as excited as me he looked very joyful as he used to be when he was a student. His wife Mina seemed very quiet and courteous as well as very matured at the same time. My friend did not change much still has the same bright brown complexion with his deep dark two eyes showed up side by side his long sharp nose. Still smiling the same way with a series of big and white teeth well even cut and beautifully arranged. He is alive with all of his smile and happiness. It took me a bit of time to accept the pretty lady as his life partner under his wide shoulder close to his wide chest. Yes! It is my friend who used to be one of my good companions six years back in the campus. Seeing him in his own place with his closest companion now beside him making me a little aloof of which I don't know why. After all it is great to see him with his wife.

My friend is talking non-stop while sitting next to his driver in the car. Mina and me mostly listening and commenting occasionally to what he has been talking about sitting at the back. He is getting louder while comparing his small city to the cities of mine of the big country once known as a dream land. He is questioning sometimes with a pause 'do you like the night city of Dhaka?' by adding again 'you don't! It's quiet and less crowded at this hour but nothing nice to view am I right?' I apologized 'no no it's good. It has its own beauty especially when it is yours.' 'You will like it when you will be able to feel the heart of the city.' Shaun is proud and shy at the same time said again smiling 'may be not. There is no high-rise building lighted at night to give you a gorgeous look actually practically you are viewing disgusting rickshaws, buses, trucks, in the streets apparently not enough wide, clean or well paved. But the good thing is now that it's not much crowded at this time at least. You'll face the traffic jam during day time. Don't blame me for inviting you here.' I think I know why he is apologizing so much and I said, 'don't worry I don't care about much about the development I know a lot about your country. Your good heart and the friendship is the heart of Bangladesh which actually pulled me here. You don't have to explain. I am enjoying your guy's company as well as the new experience here.' He paused a bit and started talking again while I took a close look at Mina sitting very calm beside me may be not even listening at all to our conversations. She looked back to me as got known that I am observing her. She smiled with a shyness as looked me in the eyes and took off her eyes again to look outside the window. I looked through the window on my side too. The car is in a medium speed crossing barriers of walls on the road side, sometimes buildings low and high rise, small or long islands, shopping malls, cinema halls, restaurants, a series of stores, clinics, or pharmacies sometimes. The rest of the areas beside are in dark while sleeping with the night time city after a long chaotic and busy day in the crowd. I have visited some places like this. All of them are congested like this.

We passed 20 min already on the way to Shaun's home. I looked at Mina again and asked 'it's late you couldn't sleep for me tonight.' 'You are our guest. I should have accompanied by Shaun its ok. Mom, dad and all others are also waiting for you. You are our guest it's a pleasure for all of us.' Added again with so much assurance 'we sleep every night. Having a guest is a blessing. We'll enjoy the night together. It happens once in a while.' Mina smiled and kept quiet again. That's a long speech of courtesy she has given ever since we met. Her smiling face shows her content and doesn't seem to be a bit curious, or suspicious or even a bit worried about anything.

On the contrary now she made me curious, very intended to see and know more of this Bengali lady apparently very pretty with all of her appearance in a nice sky blue sari with nice embroidered edges most probably a silk sari. I started to observe. She wore a gold chain by the neck, a pair of small gold drop earrings, with a pair of heavy bangles and a single plain ring all looked made of gold. All the jewelleries on the nice blue sari made her look more attractive with a very pretty face with the hair tied up as a round bundle at the back of her shoulder while a thick portion of her black hair divided into two portions over her forehead to reveal a proportionate portion by covering nicely the rest up; with two tiny and very deep eyes; with a nice shaped and well measured monument of the nose over the luscious lips with a nice pink lipstick. Overall she is skinny and very attractive with a medium Bengali height.

We got driven by a Toyota sedan through the streets or roads narrow or wide a bit, rough or smooth in less traffic at night through the series of small and cosy commercial buildings or stores, through very narrow and broken roads between very congested residential areas with houses shoulder to shoulder or some multistoried housing same way, passing by small rug tea huts open at night time most probably for the people who work late like drivers or might be for night visitors of young folks who get together at this time. There were pharmacies also on the road side especially in the residential areas. Finally, the vehicle took its turn in a nice neighborhood which looked very quiet and sophisticated comparing to some areas we passed along the way. That's the neighbourhood where my dear host resides in a big and wide flat house behind the bars of a big gate.

We walked across a moderate size garden to reach the porch. I hesitated a bit to enter the house of a family totally unfamiliar at that time without their family member Shaun also felt very guilty to bother them in the middle of the night while they all supposed to be in deep sleep. Well, the door was opened by a woman looked different in appearance as wearing the sari in a different way in comparison to the sophisticated looking bride of the house Mina. And I came to guess that the appearing lady by the door to open might be a maid of the house.

I got ashamed to see the whole family awake at around 3 am. in the morning. Very quickly I took a look at all of the members of the family were present there Shaun, his mom. His dad, his younger brother with his wife Rekha as well as Mina with some more maids and servants also smiling behind them to greet me a special guest I guess. All of them stepped forward to receive me with all greetings more from the heart rather than with a smile only. I stepped ahead to the parents who already took their sits in the living room by asking me to take a seat on the sofa in front of them. It was hard to tell how old was the mom but looked enough strong and sophisticated in a sari white in color while very nice and fine in fabric. She looked prestigious with enough light gold jewelleries and a pair of eye-glasses apparently looked very expensive with a look of sophistication of course. The father looked old enough but stronger looking in the body structure wearing a nice base suit called Panjabi as I came to know from Shaun long ago.

I looked at all in the eyes to greet them but didn't know how got confused to say 'hi' or 'hello' or to find the greetings of their own so I said 'Nomoskar!' and the both parents smiled looking at each other to corrected me very affectionately said 'it is Assa-la-mu-alaikum'. The mother started pronouncing it to make it clear to me and the father finished with proper clearance how to say and what's the meaning of it. He was almost going to preach in elaboration the mother stopped him to give me a relief may be. I remained normal but got ashamed though. Shaun's mom smiled and said at last 'hi! I am Mrs. Rebecca. How are you?' and his dad introduced himself like 'I am Mr. Sikdar. Welcome home!' Mrs. Rebecca said again 'I guess you are sleepy. You need a good sleep tonight after a long journey. We'll talk tomorrow.' Then she addressed Mina to tell the maids to do what they need to do now. Mina knew what to do she left and came back approximately after half an hour accompanied by her sister-in-law Rekha with plenty of treats carried on a trolley. The parents left before by giving orders to the maids as well as the daughters in law to take care of the guest. I already took a careful look around. The living room looked nice with all the paintings on the walls, attractive family pictures in nice frames on the walls as well. Those are the pictures of their ancestors, famous poets, favourite politicians or so as well as the very historic paintings of the world like Mona Lisa. I looked around the well-drawn curtains making the room nicely-set, well organized. A room with nice antique look sofa-set, beautiful carpet on the floor, table lamps, chandelier and big big elegant vases and sculptures present the room with good taste and elegancy.

Mrs. Sikdar appeared again while her daughters –in –law left by delivering the food. Mr. Sikdar also joined us a bit after. Mrs. Sikdar praised a lot her daughters-in-law. She seemed very proud of them said, 'my daughters-in-law are great in everything. You will know when you taste the food.' Food was delicious. The two brother's Shaun and Akbar joined also to share the taste of the delicious snacks. I was never hungry but the taste of the delicious snacks made me eat a lot unexpectedly at that hour.

Mrs. Rebecca couldn't wait for the morning to talk about some concerns she really cares about said to me 'are you also teaching?' a very start to proceed in the conversation. And as I answered promptly 'yes in the university'. 'So does my Shaun. Good, good! Very good! Then she hesitated to ask whether I was married or not when the answer was 'no', I am single' the words spread a cloud on her face and she seemed to question a lot more but didn't said only 'good, good! Very good! I believe in women's independence and freedom.' Mr. Sikdar was sitting quiet couldn't resist any more to lecture on the debate whether women should proceed independently with the speed of current mobility, rapid modernisations of human civilizations, technology, change of social behavior or outlook against all conventions family, marriage, values of individual culture and believes. Mrs. Sikdar appreciated a bit of my remarks or living single by regretting why it's not possible in their country. Mr. Sikdar condemned his wife a little for being so impractical by lecturing again on the values of cultures, morals, peace, love and happiness said 'we are human. Flesh and blood with a heart not concrete to speed up to go with the speed of an engine. We defy passion not the perfections only of the mechanism.'

Mrs. Rebecca stopped him again as usual by asking me 'what you think are women over there living better being single?' I did not know what to say or in true sense I did not want to talk over an ever continuing debate which can only results in vain. So I kept quiet for some time and expressed myself very sleepy.

After having a good dinner or snack at the end of the night two daughters-in-law were called upon their duties this time to make a bed for me along with choosing a room, showing me washroom or so. The old couple declared that they are not going to sleep anymore will say the Morning Prayer instead. We did not realize when we all actually spent the whole night together to approach the door of dawn.

The parents left and I followed Mina to the guest room. There was a double bed, a window, a single chair to a single table, a lamp on the night stand and a flower vase with some roses. For some reason I liked the room. As I looked at the window Mina exclaimed 'oops!' I forgot to open the window'. She gave me a shy smile by opening the window as if she did something wrong. And then added 'this is our simple and ordinary guest room. I don't know whether you'll be ok here or not. By the by there is a table fan. It's going to be a lot warmer later'. I was going to apologise but she did not give me a chance said 'do you mind to follow me again I want to show you the bathroom in the corridor.' I answered very promptly as if she gave me a relief by saying my need at the very moment as a guest in someone else's house. I asked 'can I take a shower now?' she got embarrassed again answered promptly as I did a while ago 'yes, of course! Why not? Feel it home. Let us know what you need.' Mina also showed me her bedroom just beside the bathroom and offered to call her any time for anything. Since the beginning I felt myself guilty for anything they did with courtesy because the timing of my arrival was very awkward so I apologized again 'oh! Yes you did not have your night time sleep yet. Must be very tired after a long day I guess. I am sorry!' 'Don't be please! It's always a pleasure. I am fine. I'll go to work late tomorrow morning. My concern is you. Feel free to ask anything. Have a goodnight'!

After performing all of her duties and formalities one of the bride groom of the house left. The maid with the miss came back to put water on the table. I looked around the room and got shocked by the sight of the window. Both doors of the window were folded on both sides but the heavy and the thick layers of the shutter blocking the view outside as well as the air. My mind strike at the thought 'to open the shutter or not' besides even confused about how to open the strong barrier over my look, my feel and my freedom to look outside from inside. A freedom lover and an open minded 'me' couldn't resist the barrier. So eventually I made it possible to be able to pull the shutter up to make my view clear and open out. The hot summer night seemed cloudy and dark with a humble humidity. There was no air conditioning inside. I could see their night garden down with a visible bloom of some little white glowers might be 'Belly' or Rajanigandha' as heard about them from no one but Shaun. A little wave of summer night cool air blowing me a little all in a sudden in my wonder's, confusions or in my thoughts at the new place to smell the nice scent of those flowers down in the garden. I decided to go to bed leaving the idea of seeing all of the garden downstairs also to see the neighbourhoods around from there.

Next day nobody or nothing woke me up didn't even know what time it was. All I felt was the very heat of the sunlight heated up my body well enough to wake me up. I blamed the sun for penetrating his naked bright raze down on me while being so high up in the sky. How much a tiny creature like me known as great as Human can hold up fighting against all the bad and barriers up and down in fact all around when the daylight can't bring a day and a cool shadow of dark cannot hide or soothe all odds to cool us down?

What was I saying? The day break of a new day in a foreign country in a friend's house as a guest. '12 o'clock! I hurried to get up to rush myself to do the first thing in the morning which is apparently finishing up the washroom job first but couldn't think of going in the small house without seeing anybody. A co-incidence or not right at the very moment the maid from the previous night showed up but of course by knocked at the door first. 'Was she peeping through the door?' thought me instantly 'how did she know that I am up? Or just waiting for me to wake up. But how did she guess me behind the door?' I thought a lot just in a single moment. But the maid entered with a lot of hesitations. She picked up the empty glass and the jug of water from the table with a silent spirit and a closed mouth gazing constantly at the same time at my bare legs down my short nighty. I tried to ignore her look but couldn't for longer. Finally, when I started feeling uneasy or shy may be she left as quiet and dumb as she entered. The air got clear finally! And I pulled myself together further by putting me in jeans again to look sober or gentle or presentable to the people of the house in a new and different environment to be accepted comfortably by them. It's a matter of adjustment to another culture and environment.

Rekha entered by knocking at the door and greeted very nicely 'Good morning!' and I joked in return for my own fault 'you mean Good afternoon?' Rekha is smart answered 'its ok it happens when you go to bed late. I think you needed more sleep for jetlag'. 'No, no I am fine for now.' I took a moment to look at her, a close look which I didn't have last night or didn't get a chance to do that. I can see now a very simple girl in Salwar- kamij as they call it. No makeup, no jewellery and most of the time looking down while talking. She looked more like Shaun's younger sister rather than a sister-in-law. While squeezing all ten fingers together she raised her eyes from the very concrete floor down to ask 'have you gotten freshen up?' mother is asking to have breakfast. She is waiting for you'.

'I am coming with you'. I said and ask her again 'where is everyone? Where is Mina and Shaun?'

'Mina Bhabhi left for the hospital. I dropped the children at school'.

'Why what happened why hospital? Is everything alright?'

'Oh, no nothing happened Mina Bhabhi works in the hospital as she is a doctor.'

'She is a doctor? Didn't know before. Do you work also?

Rekha answered only in one word 'no' and I said again like a nosey and a mean lady 'O! You are simply a house wife because you have children.'

Rekha is still assertive and also very positive in her way of talking answered 'no, I have no children of my own yet'. I stopped myself right there for being so much nosey about everybody's business especially Rekhas. I think I got it as she was taking care of Mina's children and might have a lot other responsibilities at home while Mina is not much available. I simply asked next 'what is your husband doing?'

'He is not doing anything yet trying to do some business.'

Ruling over weak is very human. I didn't know when I became a bit commanding in just a very short period of time to say 'ok! Let's go to the dining room. Take me there. Mrs. Sikdar is waiting we'll talk later.'

While proceeding through the co-ri-door I turned back to ask again 'I guess Shaun's home. Did he tell anybody that he and I have a meeting this afternoon?' Rekha's answer was humble again said 'no, but I am sure Moms know about it. They are all waiting for you.

Nobody was there at the breakfast table at that time when I got there except Rekha's husband Akbar. He was sitting at one end of the table with a lot of food in front of him. He lifted his eyes up to take a cold look at the family guest as if he didn't know me from last night's visit and took another moment to swallow the mouthful of food he had to stop chewing at the sight of the unexpected visitor right at that moment. But at least did the courtesy to say 'hi!' to get back to his course of breakfast or after breakfast meal. I didn't know myself also what would be my purpose at the dining room to take late breakfast or a course of meal in between but I was very hungry. Rekha left by reaching me there I guess to help the kitchen for late breakfast or probably to make new items for the time in between neither lunch nor breakfast. I took a seat on the other side of the table facing the TV to watch all terrible news. The beautiful lady news reader very well dressed in a nice sari with proper make-up and accessories casting all the bad news of murders, rapes, chaotic incidents, slogans of all political tensions with a very nice smile in her face all the time during the news reading. Shaun and his parents appeared to join me might be for themselves also to eat as waiting for me or woke up late just like me. Mr. Sikdar started sharing the news cast with me by explain or criticizing current incidents or social and political situations along with all the frustrations going on around the world. Mrs., Sikdar was helping me to distinguish some major figures appearing on the news as of some political figures especially.

My friend's car got stuck in a terrible traffic and I was melting in unbearable sweat. We set off for the University of Dhaka almost 30 min. ago still on the road. The car was proceeding inch by inch in the whole crowd of traffic. It was a terrible sight of the city of Dhaka at the rush hours. Sitting next to the driver made me able to see only the vast quantities of different vehicles cars, buses, mini-buses, trucks, taxis, rickshaws and also some sort of pushing huge carts with heavy goods driven by hard working folk one of them pulling from the front and two of them pushing from behind. The whole view of the roads or the streets with enormous traffic jam made the horizon horrible and unbearable especially for an alien like me in an unexpected city of ancient time or very modern with a mixture of both resulted by huge populations in a small place. Shaun is the driver today looks very restless and embarrassed at the same time and screamed all in a sudden saying 'o! Great!' and I realized that the air conditioning got unable too to cool us in the horrible heat and humidity while we were stuck in a box with four wheels hardly moving to cool us where there was no natural breeze through the windows passing across the huge crowd basically got stuck just like us between the crowds.

I looked out to give a relief to my tormented views which was trying to get an open space beyond the congested traffic. Unfortunately failed to do so. There was another kind of rush on the footpath beside the street traffic the traffic of people on feet and beyond the people jam there were small stores, open sales on the same places, hokers, buildings, low or high storied houses and so on all congested and very compact. That's not the end another crowd and chaos was there made by the children of poor class selling books and flowers by the car windows if any of them stops a little actually all the cars were mostly without a motion so the people in the cars basically suffocate themselves and captivated in the lack of fresh breathing, cooling, viewing or even thinking with a peace of mind or some comfort.

Shaun and I even lost interest to talk. He was mostly annoyed and embarrassed and I was surprised and suffocated in a superb jam with everything around. Still the sight of the little hokers gave me a break of sound thinking and a feel of love and humanity. I smiled at a lovely flower selling boy and grabbed through the window a very lovely bunch of roses offered by the boy but unfortunately failed to pay him as the car pulled forward suddenly in a speed to miss the boy behind. My sad and guilty feel got a sudden cool air by the motion along with a very nice and sweet smell of the roses. We have lots of various kinds and colours of roses grown in the fields but don't have the scent like that. Beauty and the aroma both together pointing something very excellent and natural in a place like underdeveloped Dhaka city a place with overflowing populations comparing to the neat and clean well organized spacious modern looking cities around the world.

Shaun got wrong when I cried 'oh!' asked 'what's wrong?' when I explained the situation instead of regretting he started blaming the boy 'why do they have to do things like this in so much traffic?

They should go to school'. Started blaming the system also as usual. After getting driven in the mess almost for 55 min. we reached the university area looked a little solitary and tidy comparing to those places we passed with so much hardship. The campus was big enough for the small city to accommodate. The crowd and gatherings here and there were in different shapes and moods. Boys and girls were in groups either in open spaces like fields or gardens or on the corridors as couples chatting or discussing something. Groups of girls as usually chirping like birds or chatting very loud. Some loud and cheering crowds were visible too here and there and as always I could see few of solitary or lonely students holding books to the bosom to be studious as mind their own business only.

Red brick old faculty buildings looked nice and moderate as familiar to me. I felt myself now in a real educational institution a miniature of our own. We were the part of the science faculty and reached up the department of biology by climbing stairs on time to meet the chairman of the department who led us later to the conference in another building. The thesis and the discussions I brought there was on the phenomenon of the progress or declination of modern biology was accepted with great appreciation and value for further analysis and implementation in variable matters for research and development in Bangladesh.

It was late afternoon when we finished our meetings, discussions and all. Leaving the department behind was a relief and I started to crave for a cup of coffee. But couldn't ask my friend Shaun to go to a coffee parlour or a snack-bar as I already knew Bangladeshi cultures and behaviours of the society. I did not want him to be ashamed by asking something which might make him face gossips and trouble in his relationship with his beautiful wife. It was a lovely afternoon neither too hot nor humid. We crossed some eucalyptus trees with their waves of cool breeze. This part of summer is the most favourable in a hot weather. Big trees are considered as cool shelter for travellers and pilgrims. We also passed the giant tree with a big dark green head looked like an umbrella on top of its giant wide trunk. I was trying to remember the name of the famous tree always considered as a shelter for humans under its huge and wide head of the bush and for birds into the bush. When I opened my mouth to ask my friend about the name of the tree a very common symbol of kind shelter in literature he opened his mouth at the same time to say 'are you ok? We are going to pick up Mina do you have anything to do, have something of your own or to go somewhere?' As already cut out the wish of having a cup of coffee a very simple and tiny desire but at the same time a very necessity for a break even though it's only a craving answered I 'no, no I am fine. We are going together I have no other plan.'

We were still quiet in the car while heading to the hospital where Mina works as a doctor. I was still in the thoughts of that big tree we passed through the university campus. Mina came out in a nice white and gold cotton sari. She was still looking beautiful even after work without a sign of tiredness or stress. I wondered about her smile which she kept all the time all through my visit to that small country. Shaun seemed happier, open and friendly at the reunion of all three of us again and offered us to go to a coffee or a snack bar. Mina cheered too and announced that we were going shopping after. She had to buy gifts and accessories for the upcoming wedding of a cousin of her husband.

Once again the traffic jam and the crowd to overcome to reach the destination not as bad as in the morning. The market place was the same as crowded as a mess with some people without manners or with some young students having fun or fooling around. Teasing or picking on girls seemed very favourite. Some dirty looking or perverts were also to be seen in the crowd. Those little girls and boys as found earlier in the streets also found there in the market place selling small stuffs carrying on the neck to sell from their chest on the hanging little carriages looked like as painful as their bosom to sell out some burden to the people who can pay at least a little to make the burden a little lighter. The Shaun couple remained silent all the time without making any comments or giving explanations of the scenario may be a scenario of their shame they don't want to talk about. My friends there wanted to be proud to show or point out all the new and good things to me as a foreigner. And I bought the charm of the place in a shopping place where we always refresh our souls by fulfilling our desires by spending the value we earn with hardship apart from our needs only. A wise man of whose name I am not aware of said that the market places sale our wishes only. And we buy our own wishes with hard earn money.

Mina opened her mouth first after quite a long silence in the mess of a regular unsophisticated shopping place very necessary but not nice at all. She said before entering a small store 'we'll go to a good market after we finish here.' This place is not nice but good for all they got here sometimes sell very unique products for reasonable price'. I smiled and answered very assertive 'I know we also go to different places for better deals don't worry life is more or less the same despite the time and places.' Mina seemed to be a little relieved answered again in co-operation with me.' Yes, this place is not updated and very much crowded but very well for all the accessories for a wedding. Salma will be very upset if she doesn't get all the essentials and make –ups by tomorrow. I am the one who she relies on for her taste. I got a little annoyed and ashamed for being so curious and critical about the environment over there even though I didn't say anything or make a comment on anything or even ask about anything I had been seeing but as the eyes have a language and the smile has an expression. Very quickly I replied to her as an apology for taking me there 'no, no it's fine, I like the shopping area especially when it's open like this. What can you expect more? It has an open soul.' Mina got playful to joke 'you didn't mean the mean soul of our own right?' and in return my expression as a friend got friendlier to say 'oh! Come on! Life has the same soul all around in the same globe one and only.'

'You are lovely but still you are from a well developed country which I am not.' Replied Mina again. I decided to be honest then and replied that time with some mood 'look! Life is the same with its 'goods' and 'bad' in all places only the settings, colors, manners and costumes are different. Crowds, bullies, harassments, poverty, differences, discriminations, discrepancies all these are there in developed countries to some extent in different ways. Yours are very open and visible like black and white as the differences between you and these ---------- what you say? The 'tokayees' right?' and apologized sooner right after I got ashamed for saying so much said, 'never mind' and pretended to be very happy and excited with the exclamations 'wow! Look at the gorgeous and nice saris! While entering a "Sari Bitan'.

But again got conscious about whether or not I hurt Mina's feelings by pointing out the differences. May be not Mina got busy in buying beautiful Saris, jewelleries, shining accessories for decorations and much more. That's not all she also packed some of those for me as gifts without telling me as when I was asked to choose some. What a nice manner in a friendship. Finally, Saturday morning! I was very excited about the wedding. Since the party was at noon time everyone was busy preparing themselves for the ceremony especially the ladies. Rekha spent a lot of time in dressing me up in sari. She brought a lot of them and I chose the red katan with gold embroidery she smiled and said, 'that's the color of the bride. I wondered 'O, then leave it!' she said then 'its ok red is common too. Besides the bride is the queen of the day would be in special eye catching dress up and make-up with heavy gold jewelry. You'll see lots of other ladies also wearing red but again not like the bride's one. Bride is always special.' The next moment she looked at me very curiously to ask 'are you married?' when the answer was 'no' she asked next 'you must have a boyfriend then.'

Without any hesitations I offered my photo album to show her the pictures of some nice and romantic moments of me with my boyfriend. The captured moments of love and happiness in some beautiful settings of nature and some exotic places of human civilizations. Rekha viewed them with a lot of excitements to fall apart in regret the very next moment to say 'I never had pictures like those with my husband.' I asked, 'didn't you go for a honeymoon after you got married?' She looked down and answered in a low voice with some guilt of disclosure of her secret 'no we didn't go for a honeymoon Mina Bhai did.' In a very short period of time I think I guessed the whole scenario of her marriage to point out the reality 'O! It's ok. You'll as soon as your husband get something to do like Mina and Shaun.' I know I shouldn't have gotten so quick to be interfering with their personal matters. I knew by then why she didn't have a child yet. She takes care of the house-hold, the kitchen, parents-in law and the children of the family apparently not of her own. There are maids but she is the reliable helping hand to her mother like mother-in –law. I changed the topic and asked her 'what are you wearing today?' she answered with a smile looked happy answered 'my favourite pink katan 'ma' bought it for me.' By pronouncing 'ma' the passionate word of all made me feel the family bondage while the tie between a husband - wife relationship was in doubt.

Whatever looks nice felt nice too to see the family ties are still there? Seeing her happy I asked 'was pink your wedding colour too?' she answered promptly, 'no, no it was red. I was dressed in red too.' Then I got naughty to joke a bit 'and you also looked like a queen on the very special day of the queen to enter the lock of the wedding once and for all right?' she looked me in the eyes or I can say gazed a bit and then quickly got busy to leave to take care of others and also herself at the end of the wedding party preparation. Shaun's cousin sent another car to accommodate the big family to reach the wedding altogether at the same time. Showing looked more than the reality. The grand banquet hall was very gorgeously decorated. The cars of the close relatives were decorated in red and white roses and all the cars of all others were dropping the guests or family members of the bride and the groom all dressed up in beautiful, gorgeous and special dresses both man, woman, children and all. A separate gate received us with the bride always special to view. I wondered to see all the beautiful ladies in nice dresses in different colors.

Young ladies showed up like models going for a beauty contest. The roses, the colors of the dresses, the spark of the jewelry, the decorations, the make-ups on the people, decorations on the cars and also on the monuments of the wedding banquet hall made the whole wedding picture very attractive and stunning and above all very impressive for a foreigner who basically view the picture of flood and disaster of the crowd of the population of Bangladesh. Mina was always beside me most probably enjoying my wonder and as soon as I exclaimed 'wow! Gorgeous! Etc. she replied 'night time wedding is more gorgeous, and I joked 'then I have to come again for a nighttime wedding.'

Big hall rooms separately for men and woman. The nicely decorated stage across the hallway was still barren as the couple of the wedding did not arrive yet. Two big velvet chairs as if two thrones for the King and the Queen of the day awaited in the middle of the stage. Every one once in a lifetime achieves that pride and honor or happiness exceptions also remains. In a culture like that marrying more than once is an exception and in our country remaining on one marriage is becoming a legend.

Any way it's a very exciting event for the families, friends and society people and of course a very special day for the bride and the groom with all excitements and romanticism. I took a chair near the stage where Mina, Rekha and some others got busy putting various items like sweets, a small mirror, flowers, sindur, rose water, rakhi (special hand band) and so much. Once again I was a distinct person a white sheep this time in their costume. The whiteness of my skin doesn't match with their very fair ladies. Despite the air conditioning the environment became very hot and crowded with all men, women, and children. Some kids were coming closer to me just to see me from a short distance. They watched me with wonder and I wondered at their wonder. Beautiful ladies young and elderly stopped by me with a smile and paused a bit without saying anything. Some of young folk showed some courtesy by asking 'how are you?', 'where are you from?' or 'how long you have been living here?' and 'how long you going to stay?' etc. some of the men approached to me to talk a little bit longer.

Like chatting 'I was in England once or in America for quite a longer time.' to talk about the matters in two different cultures, countries, and societies. Basically a few of them appreciated our country and its culture, its motivations with our love and faith in our own cultures, life style and so on. Good! I liked that passion.

The show was not over yet but I was kind of overwhelmed by the delicious and rich wedding feast at late afternoon. I wished to go home to sleep with a heavy stomach in the nice summer weather. All the ladies around me looked the same as drowsy as me in heavy jewels, sari and make-up. They also looked exhausted. The air-conditioning around did seem to be not cooling at all. The warm air given by the ceiling fans felt better with the humming sound of ladies chatting all around.

5.00 pm. Still nothing to do but smiling at people passing by while also noticing the differences between the outfits they were wearing. Good to see a fashion show with different beauty, different gesture and different outfits. Some of the very beautiful ladies made me feel a shame as the Bengali say 'a crow in the feathers of a peacock can't make itself a peacock.'

Things have been taking turns and twists along the way so does our lives. We travel, we move, we do trades with each other throughout the world. People always have the same heart despite the different tastes because of the different cultures. We mix together, adopt a new culture and its manners while the heart goes or follows its own ways. Making a marriage by blending two different cultures can't work out really without the blend of the taste and cultures. People pine for love and care and I don't know whether these two basic needs can make a marriage real or happy while two people desire different, taste differently or have different choices of a different background couple or of a same kind of cultures. It required a bit of debate or observations as if we say a tamed animal always goes back to the jungle where it belongs or in the contrary the portion of the water in a glass takes the shape of the glass and the portion in a bowl takes the shape of the bowl. And above all why even the almighty God created people in white, black or brown skin. The human world evolved through a lot of evolution and while still the cultural differences remains like the black, yellow and white skins over the same flesh and blood bodies.

Oh, well no need to be so much critical or judgemental enjoying the time is good enough! Good to watch the people especially the ladies all looking beautiful in wedding costumes and make-up. The way the different groups and families sitting some with children taken care by the maids some were not. Some men and women looked proud, isolated and reserve while some were not. Some of the people looked fair, some brown. Some yellow, some black within the campus of all same brown background with only some distinctions of their costumes, manners, and attitudes which is very universal in every culture. There are always mirrors within mirrors. Good hearts and good people are always the same everywhere at any status. Any way the distinct and classified people in a distinguished class with all of the man, woman, children, youngsters, or elders made the wedding environment a bit fuzzy and noisy after all had gotten observed by me with a lot of care and curiosity to make me tired and obsessed. Needed some air to get out of the buzz?

Feast was over. We got enough time to digest the heavy meal. And around 5 pm. the show time arrived for which all the people were waiting to see and greet the bride and the groom at their real wedding ritual along with a lot of fun. Finally, Rekha and Mina managed to finish the decorations and to set the couple on the stage each in a throne side by side for the first time at the very beginning of their marital reign as a queen and a king. The rest of the life awaiting for their children to inherit all.

All the guests gathered with fun and excitement to see the bridal ceremony was thrown by the bride's side mainly to humiliate the groom on their day. The reception would be thrown by the groom's party and that will be their chance to humiliate the bride's party. The bridal ceremony is called 'Rusmat'. All the guests' boys and girls except elderly people surrounded the stage to see the couple. Grooms party was climbing or peeking up to see the bride and the brides party for the groom. I proceeded myself also to the stage to see the bride and the groom along with the only lady with whom I could continue talking rather than exchanging only 'HI's or 'hello's' or a bit more like 'how are you?' by getting rid of the looks of wonder of people about me and around me.

The Rusmot seemed simple but interesting to me as it was a new and different experience to me. Al most all of the guests gathered around the stage to see what they do for fun around the couple with a lot of excitements. The people from grooms' party started picking on the bride and the brides' on the groom. Lots of laughter, cheers, and fun over the comments and teasing on the bride mainly same but a bit less on the groom of those were all joking and having fun by being socialised in a different way on the special event of a man and a woman. People were loud clapping and cheering in a huge gathering.

After the signing up of the bondage of marriage in a particular way partly religious and partly ritual the couple got to exchange flower necklace big ones with each other also got fed by each other sweets actually by others hands while also got pushed from behind while opened the mouth to have the little piece of sweet as the part of the ceremony. People laughed each time when each of them miss the piece as they get pushed from behind by people of opposite party. It's a fun and everyone wants to take turn to feed the couple.

The couple also got to exchange the 'Rakhi' the wedding band by putting on each other's hand after the ritual of having sweet and exchanging flower necklaces around each other's as if to bind each other for ever. It is a bondage to marry each other for the rest of the life. In a ritual like this people took turns to have fun, cheers and to greet the couple very loudly.

I was behind all of the people trying to get the fun by peeking and questioning the English speaking lady companion of mine for the day and got actually tired to get out of the crowd. Right then Rekha and Mina showed up from nowhere to ask me to join the rest of the fun. I stayed didn't really wanted to miss the rest of the event for my curiosity and of course my interest. The ladies brought a piece of little round mirror in the midst of all cheers. As the mirror was held against the brides face the groom had to answer the question 'what do you see?' and the groom took a mature look and smiled without an intention to say anything at all. The folk started to howl to make him say something and he just answered 'beautiful'. The crowd howled again saying 'no -------- -----say something more than all the beautiful ladies here.' He still couldn't say anything. Looked like didn't have enough spirit to joke or have fun in front of all his in-laws. A lady whispered into his ears when he finally answered 'I see a moon.' All his in-laws complained loud again 'no, no, it's daytime or as some said 'say something different' or another comment like 'our girl deserve better, and so on.

The bridegroom continued to be 'shy' on his part and just said at her turn to comment on her husband's face in the mirror 'I don't know.' The opposite party started protesting loud enough as the other party did a little while ago 'no, no---------, 'that's not an answer', and 'you cannot marry when you don't know who you are marrying.' One of the folk made a joke to have more fun 'well, Bhabhi will know well tonight to answer in the morning. Loud laughter again to say 'we won't be there in the morning' while got answered by some others 'but we can be there at night,' cheers and laughter again all loud enough to make the party cheerful and enjoyable. The "Rusmat, finished with all the fun like that. People started leaving.

I liked all those simple, silly and funny interactions if you have the mood to take part in the event for true sense. To me all those were different, interesting and a little bit funny as when I socialised myself too in the mess of all the hearts there. Those people definitely like the 'togetherness' among themselves with those kinds of fun and excitements or the charms of the costumes. I liked the bride's younger brother-in laws sense of humour who bundled up a penny in the corner of her sari to say' Bhabhi I couldn't bring anything for you except the penny.'

Finally, we reached home rushing through the warmth of the air among all we got together still with the spirit of the excitements of the party and talks about the wedding. The wedding planners were all happy said 'all went very well'. They also wished all well for the newly married couple. Well, 'all well that's ends well". Again it was just the end of the marriage ceremony not the accomplishment of a marriage. The crying scene of the wedding was like an ending scene of a drama which was definitely not a tragedy. No one else was crying except the bride and her family as she was the one who was leaving the family was born in and grown up. While I was wondering at the tragic scene of no tragedy at all. Rekha made a comment very funny 'woman cry before marriage and man cry after'. I couldn't resist my laughter. She also said 'if you be there in the morning you'll see she is arriving home with a very happy smiling face.'

Cynical me thought' it's the marriage not the wedding which can decide later who will be happy and who will be not.' The tear drops of the bride and her family members might be a little formal bur the pain they were experiencing or going to experience was real for losing a dear family member a part of it and for the bride for losing her whole world in which she grew up with all habits, tastes, desires, love, and passion. In another word her whole new life ahead is an all new start. Might be easy might be not. Human civilizations evolves with marriage to make families to continue making families to live civilized and cultured for all. Families grow in a set up to set up again by breaking into parts to make more with a new start again by breaking hearts and gluing again for good or worse but definitely for the growth of human generations or civilizations. Today's groom also was going to leave the precious part of the life to enter another might be longer or shorter in length in pain or no pain.

Later in my trip Rekha became my only close friend or a close companion through all the experiences I got in my friends Bangladesh. she was lovely, talkative, very co-operative, helping and handy as she seemed towards everyone in the family. Me and her chatting and laughing all the way towards home. When we reached home nearly an old man was sitting with a pale face with a low dignity on the tool beside the guard in the porch. Rekha's feet and mouth stopped at once at the sight of the sitting poor old man. She stepped forward with a hesitation and with a confused spirit by saying in a confused voice 'Baba!' Mrs. Sikdar stepped forward too with a lot of respect and asked the honorable in law 'why Bayai why are you sitting outside? They didn't let you in? When did you come? Is it a long time you sitting outside?' then also addressed him to come inside by scolding the guard mildly 'why didn't you let him in to sit in the living room?' she apologised a lot too with these words 'sorry Beyai, never mind these people are all nonsense!' and the Darwan didn't say anything just kept gazing at the ground under his feet.

We stepped in while Rekha made her father comfortable sitting him on a couch in the living room. Her mother-in-law continued apologising like' sorry Beyai, we were not home. Why didn't you inform us that you are coming this evening? I would arrange things for you. I am sorry! Never mind the Darwan, these people are ridiculous!' and so on. The poor dad only came to see his daughter started apologising too very very humbly 'no, no, its fine. I took the seat outside. No point getting inside while nobody's at home.' Then the lady of the house said again 'but you even didn't get a cup of tea!' she turned towards Rekha to call the maids very loud to prepare treats, tea and so on. Rekha looked at her father who came to see her after a long time seeing him into the eyes almost made her eyes watery. She pulled herself back very quickly to look at her present mom-in-law to bring her look down. Poor dad continued apologising 'its ok no need to be very busy for me. I just came to visit my daughter. I am good coming from my brother's house. They'll be waiting for me for dinner.' Mrs. Rebecca seemed a little relaxed said with comfort 'just have some snacks and tea long time no see.' And started asking about everybody in his family. At the same time asked Rekhta to take care of the goods were brought by her father without even listening to what the guest was saying about his family members. She did not hear what the dad said about her daughter-in –laws moms' health condition.

Rekha took all the goods inside by taking off her eyes from the sight of her dad. She did hear very carefully what was said about her mom and others to get enough pain inside to ache for seeing them. That was a question to be considered later in the house she is presently residing. I followed Rekha by lifting some of those without being introduced to her dad. We proceeded towards the kitchen just by then Rekha's husband got out of his room looked like just left the bed after taking a nap. I got the answer to my wonder earlier why he did not show up at the wedding while everyone else was participating. Rekha got ashamed by the sight of her husband in front of me. I know the feeling of the shame. He looked unsocial and different to me from the very beginning. Rekha and Akbar looked at each other without any language of the mouth or the eyes. He entered the bathroom and Rekha the kitchen. I didn't know what kind of a relationship they got between themselves as a husband and wife.

Unintentionally I entered the kitchen with Rekha and took a close look around. The kitchen was small comparing to the big house and its big big rooms. Two maids were there one of them cleaning big big pots and dishes the other one was preparing some food probably some quick snacks for the guest. Rekha told them to put those things away from her father while she herself set forth to put away the non-eatable items on the shelf beside the dining space. Among the two maids one was old and slow and the other one was young, pretty, quick and smart. Rekha joined the young one named kulsum in preparing the snacks. Kulsum was active and talkative asking the younger bride of the house a lot of questions about the wedding also about her dad in a dialect different from the language they speak in Dhaka. She asked 'Bhabhi, is your father going to stay tonight? When the answer was no she asked 'why?' the older one tried to stop her 'chup! You talk too much.' But kulsum was non-stop asked again 'why not? What's wrong? In our village guests stay overnight some times more.' The other one said 'people in Dhaka city go differently, live differently.'

I learned some Bengali words like 'ma', 'baba', 'thakbo', 'din,' 'rat' meaning mom, dad, will stay, day and night. As I was still trying hard to guess what they were talking about and what was explained by Rekha to the maids about her father. The picture of classifications was very obvious. The relationship between the master and the slaves is clear and common everywhere in the world. Therefore I understood the members of the house. But the relationships of Rekha and Mina with their in-laws in the house as between misses and masters of the house seemed a little subtle. These Mrs's are not maids like kulsum and again among the two Mrs.'s there was a slight differences of status as they don't get treated the same way I guess the readers already know why.

However, all of those three ladies in the kitchen were working together for the command of the house on the same floor. This time Mina was away for better and honorable responsibilities out of the congested, hot and humid kitchen with no 'exhaust' at all. Rekha was the leader there with two followers where no one fears or hesitate to follow the directions rather than 'orders'. Other than work Mina seemed more in the bed room and in the living room while Rekha was more close to the kitchen and to her 'mom' from her second family rather than the person to whom she was married. I also wondered looking at her how can a girl like her who was also with a degree be a handy person to everyone. She was also as beautiful as Mina. Then why she didn't care about herself? What kind of society or the circumstances taught her to be such selfless.

I asked her about her family, her parents and whether or not she visited them in near past. Obviously the answer was 'no'. that's what I expected as once I watched her pale face and blank eyes looking out far and far up in the sky through the glass doors at the departure of her dad by taking off her look from his back. Sometimes some moments come in our lives when we shut off our minds at the 'to do lists, to be alone to ease the pain or to cherish in the negative sense by wandering at the past, at the present with a mind full of memories or questions or confusions about the present and the future. Life goes its own way what we think, what we do and what we want do not actually co-operate with one another. The sky is open and clear sometimes, sometimes not so do our mind and soul but the questions remain with no answers for all abstracts. We are made of abstracts and the concretes but the 'self' of each of us gets always in discrepancy. We can't make things for our own or for our own choices for many reasons therefore the discrepancy can't be solved at all. Again that's also because causes can't be listed, defined or to be resolve in true sense.

Anyway I could not come to know or to see her family frequently. May be the in-laws for women maintain some family laws to decide their fate. Just wondered when the society would get rid of some restrictions or formalities or even some bindings especially for woman only. People possess power over people the question is how. Fairly they play between money, status, aristocracy. All play a very strong role in our lives so does in the difference between Mina and Rekha's life under the same roof.

Despite of critical views or the observations my visit to that place was nice, interesting and enjoyable. Rekha was spontaneous in her daily life too. Her parents –in –law were very pleased to have her specially the mother-in-law. Rekha was always nearby for any help while Mina was free to do her job, go shopping, come back home, live her life at her own convenience but still in a loose chain all by the permissions, all allowed things were being performed by her.

Any way I should not be so critical only wanted to say Mrs. Rebecca was very proud about her two daughters-in –law as if they are her own daughters as she doesn't have her own. May be I should look that way. Differences are everywhere as in one's own family where he or she was born. She talks about her two daughters with very pride one cooks very delicious food the other has a prestigious career. She seemed a well-maintained head of the family for her mood and power play. After all she is a mother her mother instinct requires Rekha for herself as she was always full of life with full of passions and emotions and above all her very helpfulness. It was Rekha and her abilities with proper education and the wit of good characteristics brought her close to her mother-in-law believed to be half of her own mother in the later half of her life. This young lady seemed a lot practical to know how to live in a social structure. She used to be respectful and confident said once 'I am like her own daughter that's why she doesn't want to lose me. Besides Bhabhi is outgoing and always busy. Someone has to be with her besides her maids. My mom says 'husband and his family is the real family of a girl.'

Women get shifted from one family to another from the roots to another set up to make a new family. Cultures evolve, families grow, societies prosper but a marriage remains unhappy and unfulfilled sometimes like Rekha's. Well, all flowers don't reach the bloom we don't care but the One who does create might care with full respect we can't think have how, when and where. There is still society, divinity and love in these institutions for the good for mankind.

My visit to Shaun's place almost came to an end. Funny I came to see Shaun along with his Bangladesh but became very conservative about the family, the society, the nature of the society and above all Rekha representing women of all time in a new costume to me and also in an new environment, culture and the circumstances they create. Rekha became my main companion instead of Shaun if I am a spectator through my journey to a new land. She accompanied me all the way to live, to enjoy, to relax, to talk, to think, to learn and share in my acceptance of the family as a comfortable place to make my own with beautiful people in a shorter period of time.

There was nothing to see actually in the old town an unimpressive and congested city of Dhaka except the differences comparing to the developed cities. Shaun and Rekha offered me a lot to see places like the zoo, parks, and amusement parks or market places. The zoo was not that bad comparing to a zoo in counties like ours. They also have enough collections of wild life. It was always nice and mouth-watering to go to a market or shopping place. All the items they sell used to attract me a lot as they were new with new looks and materials. Was also very good to enjoy all delicious food outside. The Mina bazar was stunning with the girls and beautiful ladies all dressed up nice for showing. A small country with different beauty with little rivers, greens, valleys, delicious food, was really stunning to visit the old city of Dhaka and walking on the bank of Buriganga. I felt the heart of the people accompanied with me as well as the heart of Ganga with its gentle cool breeze in hot. All of us Shaun, Mina, Rekha walked in the very old streets until late night. People in that place in small restaurants in the streets or wherever did not look gentle at all but somewhat capable of influence the strangers with the touch of their hearts expressed in their humble and innocent behaviour and attitudes to the people like me. They care, they set forth with the expression of their bosom seemed very touchy to visitors whom they normally do not see. My heart felt like touching theirs and my feelings felt like mingled with theirs. It was like a magic of a touchstone in a new place. The fun park seemed nothing but a miniature of what we got here in our country.

By visiting the places of Dhaka, staying with Shaun's family and visiting his friends and family along with all of his relatives I got enough knowledge of an underdeveloped small country Bangladesh but after all I got depicted a picture in my mind of the hearts of its people in their relationships even with a foreigner like me. They know how to feel, how to love, how to live and love and cherish all they got little or insignificant in the midst of all of their struggles for survival.

Anyway my curiosity was to see Bangladesh my great friends Bangladesh an insignificant, small and poor, a small piece of land on the globe. I believe life is precious and valuable above all. I see values of cultures, beliefs and virtues over all the vices in the existing societies lived by people definitely human anywhere on the globe in the lap of Nature.

I also wished to see the villages there outside the city of Dhaka. Shaun's plan to visit his village got cancelled because of the flooding there and

Rekha's proposal to take me to her small rural town got rejected too by Mrs.Rebacca as it was not a good timing. The rural areas are not as beautiful as overwhelmed by its overwhelming beauty. I viewed the villages or the rural areas a lot of time. They are green with woods, ponds, rivers and lakes, vast lands of gold or green in different seasons, fruit gardens in some places or vegetables. People live in houses of hay, tins, or some other materials other than bricks surrounded by woods mostly. People like kulsum live by the banks of the river or the sea shore to be stricken by natural disaster to end up their fate in town mainly in the city of Dhaka. Rekha came from a small town near Dhaka a small city with still educated people with some trades and business. According to Shaun villages in Bangladesh touches his heart. They are not vast neither do well maintained but beautiful with all of Nature to breath from hearts to hearts.

Beautiful night. One more day left for me to live, to enjoy, to see a foreign land. That day passed with a lot of fun outside in the city with Mina and Shaun by going shopping, spending time in an ice-cream parlour, movie theatre and a Chinese restaurant. The day was also nicer in the summer season as if the weather put mercy on me by making the summer time heat less and by spreading a nice breeze through my farewell. Sitting at the balcony at that night didn't really know what was there waiting for me to experience. What surprise as a gift waiting for me to take with me from that land. I was still watching the light dark open sky up preparing its cloud for a cry out or for a blast. I was still in a romantic mood enjoying the weather.

About 2. Pm I got up the chair on the balcony to go inside when I saw kulsum taking off the dry clothes from the hanging ropes in the garden down in the backyard. As I heard Mr. Rebecca calling her loud. She ran inside quickly with all the clothes. Then came back again and entered the small house in the corner out in the garden. I wondered what's there in that tiny little house most probably a storage or a log house. I stopped there for some more time not knowing for what. Might be for the rain. The sky already started to cry to give me a good feelings from her bosom by the beauty of her showering. A bit later while looking at the rainfall with its rhythms I noticed that Rekha's husband who was also my wise friend Shaun's brother Akbar also coming out of that storage house. I got curious and waiting for kulsum to come out.

Someone touched my back with a gentle hand to bring me back to look back. It was Rekha she looked pale. I got surprised to ask 'Rekha? You didn't sleep yet?'

'No couldn't sleep. Can't sleep.'

'Are you always like this?' I asked.

'Most of the nights.'

She answered and with a little pause said again 'sometimes I come to this room some nights to have a sound sleep.' Then I joked 'I guess I took your place and who is taking yours?' but got guilty at the same time for hurting her feelings. Felt myself a fool at the same time got stunned to see Rekha gazing at me with a stoned look to answer to my stupid question said 'no, one can take my place!' very strongly. I tried to make the air lighter and started to talk about her nice sari 'nice sari! You look beautiful tonight! Where did you get this sari?'

'My mother-in-law bought for me. She buys everything for me.' I knew Mina was independent Rekha was not. Mina had choices Rekha did not. May be she didn't even try to be or might be she was not even allowed to set forth on her own. She looked dedicated to the family where she got married in or was chosen to be dedicated to the family in the business of matrimonial institution. I kept quiet for a bit of longer time as if I took a pause to feel her pain and she took her time to shed off her sorrows in the tranquility of the night in the company of a very stranger from a country far far away. From all of her stories I felt her deep emptiness inside a childless and a companionless marriage ironically being with her very legal life partner very close under the same roof. A pointless therefore a lifeless marriage didn't really make any sense to me. Her marriage might be pointless but definitely not to her. It was valuable to her might be still as it gives her enough value to feel pain to gain something out of it which can only be a relationship of love,care,passion and a desire to make a real home.

However, those are only my concerns I believe. Who cares now-a-days besides she speaks less and works more definitely for others not for herself? Sacrificing woman and their wishes on the alters of human society of which they are the equal portion of man is not new never was actually it is very legendary. They were needed to be sacrificed for good in the past and still are driven or being to be scarified by themselves in the cultures, behaviours and systems of the societies. They get tortured or deprived of or even killed still in the present social structure which are still no less superstitious or very demanding for women only. Gods always rule and goddesses get testified for love, purity and values. Hindu Goddess Sita had to be testified in the fire to get back her love for no reason at all. They are being testified for everything in life for a family, for love, for a settlement in life or even just to live a life with respect and in comfort.

The Great One above who settled everything with the creation of the universe and mankind by dividing them into two inseparable parts man and woman. Who is great who is not, who is more important who is less, who is more powerful and valuable who is less remains always for debate but treating woman the way they have been treated by man or by the society which includes woman also is beyond understanding might be even by the Great who gave all the senses of judgement. Manmade societies apparently set forth for values to live a civilized life for good for all at the same time started falling for certain beliefs and superstitions to dominate woman only. Great poet Tagore's 'Hoimanti' dies at the altar of so called society which contains indoor world ironically consists of women where the newly wed Hoimanty couldn't survive. What makes women to kill or torture another woman like them? Why the social behaviour and outlook never change at all until now.

Woman became victims suffer half of their life and make the new-comers suffer same way on the same platform might be thinking right and just or just to be jealous to avenge their pain and emptiness or failure to get what they needed to get and to achieve what they wanted to achieve. Avengers might even don't know that they are ruining the blooming of the new to blossom. Victims victimise, powerful possess, consumers consume for pleasure, players play, enjoy and destroy eventually then who value and respect these objects considered to be womankind. Only those women deserve values and respect by means of money and status.

So, this is reality. Independence or economic independence can make women move forward only but can't give them a real life as I said man woman as partners for real life together. Then who will come to break the chain. As I mentioned before about the abstract things in our lives love, feelings, passions, emotions, friendships, can't be possessed or controlled but humanity can.

At the silence of a silent night time Rekha came to my room a very silent woman ever to depict a picture of her tormented heart and mind only with a very few words. I kept silent too without bothering her by asking anymore personal questions. Both of us kept quiet for quite a bit of time until Rekha sighed loud from her bosom and eventually as I was going to say something we heard her husband yelling very loud. Both of us hurried downstairs. Rekha's life partner and kulsum's sex partner was yelling at both kulsum and his mother. Both mother and her brave son forgot about the presence of the guest in the house while arguing loud enough with each other. I couldn't read what words they were exchanging towards each other a spoiled son and a poor mother. The subject Kulsum happened to be the guilty of the black scene of the dark night standing in between with enormous fear and guilt in her shattered eyes. The guilty bull of the house was still shouting at kulsum by calling names to cover his real name. He got almost mad to threaten her to beat up if she didn't leave yet said to the mother screaming loud 'kick her out! Kick the bitch out! Can't bring her own sin on me. Bloody bitch will ruin all our honor'. The mother did not waste anymore words on her son and told kulsum to pack up to leave in the morning.

The insignificant poor little 'thing' didn't really have anything to say except to cry to accept the consequences of the situation even though it was not totally her fault. Who care about these poor 'things' feel or think or what go on in their heart in such a crisis like this. Victims let their honor go if they have any according to our concern and keep the honor of the victimizers by putting themselves in misery, uncertainty by throwing themselves into the lap of the fate if only fate can put mercy on them like kulsum who has to leave now the little job for her survival and shelter. They do mistakes normally considering the masters hold or might be sometimes for their own foolish fantasy if these little things have a little heart to wish. Working class supposed to serve the rest merely by working out the body to feed and keep the body alive to live a life with no meaning, no aim just to 'stay alive.'

Rekha was still quiet just beside me whom I totally ignored for the past hours didn't really have curious to see her reactions over Kulsum's fate or her very dear husband's great behaviour. The mother of the 'hero' or the 'villain of the scene calmed down after finding a solution of letting the maid go to get rid of the scandal forever and got relaxed to take a chair in the kitchen. What can she do except to accept the fact was caused by her own son? I guess, I guessed right about what happened. Her brave son came down too and went close to his mom like a little boy asking for food got really hungry after a noble fight and a noble decision to make very wisely for the family honor by casting away the odd of his own. The mother and the son sat together in care and affection again. Instead of Kulsum the other maid served some food in the very odd time for the cause of an odd situation. The chaotic night cooled down finally doesn't matter what would be the consequences for who. Some loose some gain in a game but in a live drama of real life winners and looser are all in discrepancy hard to define the true meaning of loss and gain in the moral sense actually.

I looked at the re-union of the mother and the son usually a beautiful scene but not at that moment. I always looked at them in that family as Rekha was never together with her husband not even around him. She and Akbar both are actually around the mom together or individually serving the mom or the mother-in-law. It was always Kulsum or the other maid serving food for Akbar instead of Mrs. Rebecca not Rekha for her husband. I never saw Rekha with her husband together for any reason. If the mother was not there the big boy eat his meals all alone. He used to be either relaxing himself or helping 'mom' with lot of things. Unlike Akbar and Rekha Shaun and his wife seemed to be a romantic couple and the younger ones were totally in contrary.

Both Rekha and me looked at each other by looking at the mother son relationship and left the spot for thunders and storms of family emotions. We were heading towards the stairs. Before stepping up I looked back again at Kulsum standing in a corner downstairs very guilty and down. I did not have anything to think of her what fruit the bushes produce down the big trees of fruit no one really cares. Still out of the suspected cause of the drama that night I whispered to Rekha 'is she carrying?' Rekha tried to deny which could not be denied whispered back to me to utter 'yes!'

We both went upstairs very silently and kept silence again for longer time coming back again to the guest room. Rekha kept looking outside the window and I grabbed her diary sitting there on the table since the very first day of my arrival at the house.

'Can you tell me folk, which one is better a life in death or a death in life?

Or what even could be the difference?'

'If berries are berries
What's the purpose the wild bushes carries?'

'Why the fish jump up to fall?
Big are Big of them all?
Who stamped them after all?

Makes the smalls for Big
To be cherished by them all?'

"Catherine!'

'Yes, Rekha?' I closed her diary hastily and said 'sorry I read a little of your rhymes.'

'It's ok. She replied shortly.

It was really late but none of us really wanted to sleep. Looking at her pale and sad face I put Kulsum beside her with the same pain in my imagination to compare the Miss and the maid in a very sophisticated family probably well known in the society. And asked with a caution intended not to hurt her at all 'are you happy here?'

'Why?' she questioned instead of a straight answer looking into my eyes carelessly.

'I mean do you have a relation with Akbar? Did you ever sleep with him?'

'I sleep in his bed not with him.' Her short answer again but very pointy.

'Why? Because you don't like him?'

'Yes, he is not competent to me while I am not competent to his Family.'

'Then why did you marry him?'

'My parents have three more daughters to marry.'

As I gazed at her significantly to ask 'do they have to?' she was still strong enough to defy me said, 'yes, for their future. We can build up ourselves but we can't make a new society in a new frame.'

'So you decided to sell yourselves?'

'It's better to be sold to a family rather to be sold in the market.' again she is firm and very practical under circumstances.

I felt all her pain with all my heart to console this way 'its O.K. Women's condition is more or less the same everywhere. It's a long time since you got married did you ever love him?'

'I don't know what love is I only feel bad and suffer when he goes to those women. He can't really embrace me for love he likes me around as a family member around his family.'

'Very strange? May be one day time will change you guys to make you a bondage.'

Almost three weeks passed quickly didn't even gave myself a pause to look back what was there in my own place, what are the things to be done after going back. Just got carried by the flow of all visits to places in viewing, tasting, enjoying, observing and wondering at all new and strange things of a new land. The time arrived finally to pack and leave. Kulsum left by packing up all burdens including one in her tummy and I am leaving a dear friend and his family and all of his surroundings with a lot of memories and endurance from the visit. Leaving with a pain with gain will miss all the love, friendships and care. All the memories of good time, good weather in all the visits all together. And also all the observations of the culture and societies of Bangladesh for all of its fun, beauty and rituals as well as all the bindings and shortcomings as the core of cultures in an undeveloped country like Bangladesh. Well, definitely will miss a lot for its all beauty and all differences. The change and newness I got here was never forgettable. I'll miss Rekha, I'll miss Shaun, I'll miss Mina and all the memories of joy and pain with joy and pain together. Meeting Rekha might be revolutionary as she made me put focus on women all around the world along with the societies where we reside.

8 pm Friday, I am packing here everyone else are out shopping except the elders and Akbar as usual. They planned a lot gifts to buy for me while I have no room in my suitcase. Let's see how much room I can make tonight for them by shedding off my gifts for them.

Good night! The clock is ticking 9 more hours to leave my dear Bangladesh. Good night all again all.

----------------- THE END

www.ingramcontent.com/pod-product-compliance
Lightning Source LLC
Chambersburg PA
CBHW070450170726
48291CB00005B/1682

* 9 7 8 1 9 4 9 7 4 6 6 7 9 *